The Sinner Has a New Address

The Sinner Has a New Address

Jackie Bean

Published by Seemore Bean Publishing

Printed in the United States of America

To contact the author or order additional copies:
1jackiebean@gmail.com

First Edition, 2019

ISBN: 978-1-7928306-6-2

Library of Congress Control Number: 2019900062

Front and back cover photos from Adobe Stock by Tono Balaguer

Content editing by Nikki Busch (nikkibuschediting.com)

Copyediting by Judi Orefice Heidel
(perfectlycleareditingservices.com)

Cover design by Mi Ae Lipe (whatnowdesign.com)

Interior design by Julie Klein (JKlein-Editor.com)

DEDICATION

In loving memory of my Mom and Dad. There were no parenting books and I still turned out okay. To the man who loved me and whom I loved back: to be continued. To my friends: without you, I would be laughing at my own jokes. To E.C. Murray: you believed in me!

The mind will not always remember
exactly what happened but the heart will
always remember the feeling.

— BRIGITTE NICOLE

CHAPTER ONE

"It's Juliette to you, Sister Mary Elizabeth. My name is Juliette, not Jules." The Sister's bulging eyes peer down at me; my head is pressed painfully against the flat wall. My teary, salty blue eyes glare purposefully back at her. I should be afraid. I am a little, but God is the only one who knows for sure. How dare I challenge the official creed in catechism class? Love is the fundamental and innate vocation of every human being. It does not exist only between a man and a woman. I believe in love. Solid, devoted love between men and women, gays, or lesbians—love is love.

"Sister, have you ever loved another human being, a partner who is a part of you, the one who brings calm to your soul, seals your heart with love, frees you from all fear?" I ask.

"God is my partner. Anything else you would like to say, Juliette?"

Knowing that no response is expected, I sit in pure silence, unworthy to be in her presence. Her ruby-red cheeks on fire, she chokes inside her habit. Her squinting eyes talk to me with what I imagine to be scolding words, and she lifts her black wings, pointing the ruler at the door. I stand, head held high, and count my steps to the door. I open it quietly and close it even more quietly behind me as I enter the darkness of the hallway.

I slowly slide to the floor, my back against the solid concrete wall. My feet are planted firmly on the ground, and a chill travels up my legs from the cold tile floor. Crossing my arms to warm my body, I sit still.

The door next to me opens. Do I dare look up? Quickly it slams closed. The black fabric slaps me in the face; the laced black shoes dance around me. Focusing my eyes on my feet, I don't dare look up. As I slowly tilt my head, my gaze follows the black holy cape flying down the hall until it disappears into the sunbeams shining down from the heavenly high stained-glass window.

I fixate on the clock below the window, watching the second hand crawl toward the twelve. Counting down in my church whisper . . . ten, nine, eight, seven . . . amen, five, four, hail Mary, three, two, until . . . ring, bells dance in my head. My leg muscles pulsate with prayers, and with one last amen, I stand up on quivering legs. I stroll leisurely toward the exit sign, never losing sight of the heavenly gate. I pause for a second at the doors before my soul's strength pushes them open to my newfound freedom. My back to the church, each step is filled with more confidence. Under my breath I whisper one last alleluia.

I scan the parking lot. Cars are filled with patient parents waiting for their divine adolescents. I squint frantically in search of the forest-green family Chrysler. The heat from the midmorning sun shines down on my face, and I shield my eyes with my hand. I see the car parked off in the distance. Standing up on my toes, I stretch my hands high above my head and wave my imaginary SOS flag to get my mother's attention. Mom waves to me out the window, and the car rolls in slow motion. The crackling sound beneath the tires gets louder as it crawls across the heated blacktop. Moving toward her, I fill the gap, grasping for the heavy metal door handle before the car comes to a complete stop.

"Jules, you can wait until the car stops to get in."

"Not today, Mom."

I duck my head into my escape car, and my backside follows, tumbling down onto the fabric front seat. Static shocks send waves of energy from head to toe. I stomp the floorboard with my feet.

Mom's gradually pressing on the gas pedal. She waves out the window. "Nice to see you, Ruth. We need to catch up soon." Her head leans out the window a little bit farther to talk some more.

Trying to get her attention back to me, I deepen my voice and slap my hand on the dashboard. "By God, this is important, Mom!"

She slowly pulls her head inside the car and turns to me, one eye on the road. "Catechism is over for me. These baptized feet will never enter another Catholic

Church. And one more thing, Sister Elizabeth will be calling the home phone. Tell her my name is Juliette, not Jules." A smile bigger than the Bible Belt covers my face.

My body is reacting, heating up from my interaction with the higher power. I need air. Why can't I just sit in class and accept what they teach? I grab the window knob, rolling it feverishly round and round. The glass window slowly lowers and disappears; the wind cools my face. I grip the soft fabric seat below me and push myself up and off my seat, but the seat belt jerks me back into the car. More slowly this time, I gradually stretch my body out the window. My neck muscles strain, and the wind lifts my hair, swirling it away from my face. I close my eyes. With my head hanging out of the window, my shoulder rests against the door. Sluggishly I open my eyes and roll my head back. I watch as the church disappears. It doesn't look so mighty anymore. I pull my head back inside the car. Wanting to look in the mirror, I drop the sun visor. "Wow, what a holy mess!"

Thank you, Sister. I did learn something in catechism. I have a voice. You awakened me by trying to silence it. I will pray that I find the love that brings musical angels and calming spirits. My soul partner exists out there. I am not afraid in this limitless world. My voice will be heard, my thoughts will be shared, my life journey lies before me. I will find the person whom I will love until my last breath.

Junior year of high school starts in three days. School tortures me with the cliques and hurtful gossip and make-believe friendships. Teens crowd the malls in search of new clothes to show their style; colored hair and trendy cuts make them look older and wiser. The newest fashionable shoes lift us high to match our visions of success. All of it is trivial to me, and a waste of effort and time. My true girlfriends make me smile; my arms are always open to them, and vice versa. They are my lifelines as we trudge together through our awkward teen years. At the age of sixteen, we have all the answers, but I'm not sure we know the questions.

CHAPTER TWO

My parents work hard at our family-owned business in downtown Cleveland. I recognize tired eyes and swollen, sweaty feet from long hours of standing. Work shifts are split between Mom and Dad to keep the bar and restaurant operating smoothly. The pride of ownership comes with sacrifice to my family, and most of our Sunday afternoons are spent together at the restaurant — cleaning, restocking, and painting.

The smell of grease and spilled beer permeates deep into Mom and Dad's hair and skin. Their clothes reek of grilled onions and charbroiled burgers — it's the smell of hard work, at least that's what they tell me. One parent is always home with us, my sister and me. I have three sisters. Marcella and Grace are married but live a short drive away in neighboring towns. Jane is two years older — bound by blood, split by individuality, a pain in the ass, we both would say. We love each other in a hair-pulling, cat-fighting kind of way.

I am the baby in the family, sister number three. Given the fifteen-year age gap between us, I don't think my parents planned on another child. I am loved, coddled, and sometimes just tolerated, with a tired eye, by my parents.

Game boards, cards, and whoopee cushions fill the house on any Sunday. I love my mom and dad; they are filling my childhood memories with summers at the beach, weekend ski trips to Vermont, and competitive games of lawn tennis on our court in the backyard. I am sixteen years old, it's 1979, and I spend my daydreaming time planning my future. I may be too young to know what I want to do, but I do know what I don't want to do. I wonder what new experiences I will have. My sisters describe me with red caution, possibly with emergency flares, while I search and find my own sorts of thrills with my friends. Words like reckless, free, spoiled, irresponsible, irresistible, and independent fill their descriptions. I laugh just thinking about laughing.

I rest my bony butt on the faithfully polished pews on Sunday mornings, daydreaming of a better place to be. I never feel comfortable in this house of hymns; my stomach aches watching the swinging censers pollute the air. I cover my nose with my arm, trying to breathe through my clothes. Mom tugs on my hair locks, slowly lifting my head out of my shirt sleeve, sending the signal to knock it off and straighten up because the church bells are ringing; the show is about to start. The spreading perfume smells linger, bells ring, the organ music stops, we all rise.

Lies will kill friendships, religion is a close second. Don't tell me what God told you to do or wants me to do. He didn't tell you anything — the bible is just a book, and I have a hard time believing the meaning of the words inside. If you believe unrealistic words and interpretation of stories changed over time, do not expect me to follow. If your book of God says a man can walk on water and a virgin can have a baby, and you believe it, don't ask me to take you seriously. That Sister or priest who is giving advice about love and relationships? Now come on! They have devoted their love to a character in a book. You cannot give advice from teachings in a book — that's outrageous and contagiously funny to me — a bad habit.

My girlfriends worry about their boyfriends, the dates, and the dances. I worry about trying to keep track of their weekly dose of dating and drama, observe as they overdose on emotional, dramatic binges. Boys are their drug; they are the addicts. They want more. More attention, more acknowledgment, more, more, more. They live; I learn. Through them, I watch life lessons, live and in full color. I am solo in real time.

It is Friday night; the summer of 1979 is coming to an end with a hometown party. We dress in our trendy summer-flowered shorts, bright-colored tank tops, and sandals that are salty from our family summer vacations. It's Cindy's turn to drive. We jam into her dinged-up honey-yellow Toyota Corolla, our arms and legs overlapping. Tonight, we pave the way to end the summer. Makeup mirrors reflect our innocence as we roll the last touches of lollipop-named lip gloss across our lips. The finale of summer, this party introduces new dating prospects for my girlfriends, which will then be followed by more therapy sessions for me to lead. The broken heart, the cheating-teen drama, all play out for me to watch.

Music booms from the car radio, and we belt out the words to the popular song "Any Way You Want It" at the top of our lungs. We are an orchestra out of sorts. Clapping, tapping, our heads bobbing with our mouths wide open, we sing out the words with beaming smiles, our air guitars strumming the last strokes as the song's end is near.

The yellow beater crawls sluggishly down the party street, the car shocks tested by the swaying bodies inside. With Cindy's foot barely touching the gas, we cruise, searching for an open spot in the long line of parked cars along the road. Car windows rolled down, sun setting on our faces, at the top of our lungs we finish singing the song, with sketchy melody and a hint of harmony.

Screaming above the singing voices, I yell, "Stop, there's a spot."

With a quick turn of the wheel, Cindy maneuvers the car into the tiny opening. When she slams on the brakes, the car slants into the brush and our bodies nose-dive forward.

"Everybody out. Let's go light up this party," Cindy says.

The front doors fly open and lanky arms and legs appear out of the backseat, limb by limb, evacuating the car.

"Fix your hair — it's doing weird shit."

Casually I run my fingers through it. "Whatever."

Our outfits tethered down to cover excessive skin, we check makeup and hair in the parked car's rearview mirror and weave down the middle of the paved road to the party.

Following the trail of arriving partiers, we slide our sandals through the damp grass. The sound of the music gets louder. The setting sun has swallowed up the daylight hours, and the evening dew sweeps in. We hover close, walking quietly along the dimly lit pathway to the back of the house.

"Watch your head."

Hunched forward, ducking under tree branches, I notice the last of the summer leaves clinging for life. It's three steps up to the wooden deck, and there the heartbeat of the party is laid out before me. I pause at the threshold to observe the sights ahead. Energy radiates back to me, the music beating fast and loud.

"This is it, the end-of-summer party. The start of a new school year is around the corner," I say.

A mass of teens is spread across the sprawling yard, some gravitating toward the mountainous bonfire, which is about to be lit, while others line up at the keg.

My love-hungry friends scatter fast like ants, traveling swiftly, looking for a feast between blades of new grass.

I call out to them before they start nibbling on their next dessert. "Hey, guys, let's meet back up in an hour, right here on the deck."

"Sure."

"Okay."

I give them a thumbs-up and watch them drift deeper into the sea, the tops of their heads disappearing as they bob into the crowd. Familiar faces pass by me, inquiring casually about my summer.

"What's up, Jules? Have a good summer?"

I turn slowly to meet their gazes. "Awesome."

"Bummed summer is over, that's for sure," my softball teammate says.

"The team is chilling just on the other side of the keg. I'll see you over there." I point into the darkness, my eyes following my finger. "I see them over there, sounds like a plan. Heading over there after I grab a beer. Going to surprise those posers."

I pump my fist in the air, keeping time with the vibrant music, and I stride fast toward the keg and find my place at the end of line. Fifteen deep we stand, shuffle forward, wait, shuffle forward, and wait some more. I tap my foot, the music making me sway my hips as I tiptoe ever so slowly forward in line.

"Save me a dance tonight, Jules." Kerry slides by, methodically rubbing his hand down my back.

"Catch me later, Kerry." Man, is he good looking. Am I stupid or what to reject that?

Finally, I am at the front of the line. The bubbly brew fills my red Solo cup to the brim, the frosty head teetering on the edge. My lips separate slightly around the rim, and the cold beer runs over my tongue and down my throat. Twisting and twirling on my toes, I weave my way toward my softball team. We rub backs, knock knees, and hand out high fives until I pop up in the middle of the group.

"A toast. Here's to —"

"Hey, look who we have here, an almost pitcher," the team captain says, cutting me off midsentence.

"Aw, come on, I got feelings, ya know. Nah, just kidding! Eat shit and die. A toast to 1980's upcoming season. Let's pray I can throw mores strikes this year."

Laughter erupts, and I try to steady my quivering body with a sip of beer in honor of my own toast.

Under my breath I say, "Oh, please come true."

Beer spills over the cup, dribbling down my chin. I wipe my face with my jacket sleeve.

"I missed you this summer. Gotta love my smartass jocks," I muse.

Trash talk flows around the circle. No one is safe from abuse.

"Remember the game you walked in ten batters?"

As they rub salt into the memory bank of bad days on the mound, my body stings with pain. A smile on my face, I replay that day in my head and how they picked me up when I couldn't pick myself up after the game.

"I'm outta here. Someone out there might be recruiting pitchers."

Aimlessly walking on the deck, away from my jock clique, I peer above the crowd, balancing on my toes, hoping to spot someone from my carpool.

"Good luck out there. Let us know if you get drafted by another team." The circle erupts in laughter.

Turning my head slightly, I yell back to them, "I get it. I get it. The goal is to throw the ball over the plate!" More giggling erupts behind me.

On the deck, one hand placed casually in my shorts pocket, the other holding my beer, I look around to find my feisty ants out in the pool of plenty. With no one in the carpool in sight, I settle into my surroundings and scope out the sea of intoxicated jubilance and laughter.

Who is that? The pretty face, the perfect body! Someone new. A hum vibrates in my chest. Flames of awakened passion have me exploring this stranger with dizzied eyes, dissecting each precious body part, one by one. Who is this little piece of heaven on earth?

Feet steady, my body anxiously bending to get closer to him like a tree blown by the wind, I hope to grasp the sweet sound of his voice or the joyful ring of his laughter.

Calm reigns over my body. I am in an ocean, my head above the water, floating effortlessly in the salty waves.

Have we met before? Friends of friends? Dissecting him from head to toe, surely I can find a flaw in his polished physique. I note his toned torso beneath his white-collared polo shirt. Damn, no beer belly. Still pleased at what I am looking at, I am drawn to his quadriceps. Athlete, I assume. My cheeks warm, and a fever builds in my body while

I take in this new sight. Suddenly I am way too hot in my summer outfit.

Entranced by his slow, strategic movement and precise gestures, I watch his every move. He raises his right hand to welcome a newcomer into his circle of conversation, offering a strong but gentle handshake. His muscular biceps perk up, and his hand spreads wide to welcome his guest. Beer in hand, he slowly brings it to his lips, the cup's rim resting on his bottom lip. He tilts it up, allowing the cold brew to coat his throat. I lick my own lips, imagining myself licking his. He smiles at the newcomer and his cheeks rise. I imagine his words of greeting are calm and gentle. Maybe a "hello" or a "nice to meet you." Mesmerized by his muscular structure, I want to know him, yet it's so unlike me to spend this much time on a stranger.

The bonfire is piled high with large branches, twigs, and firewood, the top teetering with empty beer boxes, the crowd anticipating its burst of brilliance. With all eyes on the pile, the strike of a match sends flares of reds, oranges, and blues into the darkness. The crowd erupts with excitement, singing a chorus of oohs and aahs. The lighted brilliance reflects in the whites of their eyes. The scorching, hot flames build in size, and everyone takes one giant step back as the smoke blows in different directions. It fills my nose with smoky incense.

The night sky collides with the roaring flames of light, the heated beacon rising toward the moon.

Solo cups are held high and alcohol overflows from bottles to cups all around him. Song and cheer erupt from the new choir linked arm in arm, swaying to the music, circling the bonfire. A drunk rendition of a Rolling Stones song devolves into mumbles from the crowd, the sound rising through the smoke to the heavens. Obnoxious drunken song and the hum of chatter echo off the tall trees enclosing the backyard.

Pure virgin silence is in my brain, filtering out the useless noise that surrounds me. I am bobbing in waves of calm as I look at him. My thoughts are simple, my breath shallow. Watching, in awe of this stranger, I wonder who this person is who has warmed my heart, lit my body on fire, calmed my brain, and taken me to a place I have never been before.

"Hi, Jules. How are you?"

Jumping back, shaken by this interruption to my daydreaming my eyes never leave my prize. I lift my hand in acknowledgment.

"You look great! Good summer? Ready for school?" A schoolmate is trying to engage me in conversation.

After I move my head up and down in voiceless answers, the unacknowledged soul moves on.

Did he feel the gaze of my eyes, the heat of my body? His head slowly turns away from his conversation. Our eyes meet, tangled in muted exchange, majestic vibes of a different kind unlocking my padlocked heart, mysteriously opening the combination. Soaking all of him in, the edges of my lips rise, forming a beam of friendly tenderness. As I enjoy this steamy, amorous connection, I want to reach across the lawn to touch him. He is smiling back at me. Motionless, we engage, lost in conversation, no translation needed. We have a connection, and I relish it in silent pleasure as the timeless conversation goes on vibrating the universe.

In slow motion, his head turns away. Untethered, my lungs deflate, our connection broken. I come back to reality.

What the hell, jerk? Why did I waste my time on you!

Our harmonious connection is gone. My eyes close, my head hangs low, my chin touches my chest. I regret letting my guard down. Strands of blond hair plunge forward, shielding disappointment. Teary eyes stare at the green grass below my shoes, nostrils flare. The winds blow in barn-burning directions. They seem to be just as hot and confused as me, filling my lungs with the smoky air.

Locking my heart back up, I raise my head, lean back, and shake my head, the silky blond strands unfurling evenly across my shoulders, washing away rejection.

What an emotional rollercoaster. I roll my head around and around, loosening the strained muscle tension, my neck crackling. Unbuckle me from this ride that threw my heart around. *Sister, what did you teach me? Apples set an eternal curse?*

I bolt in the direction of erupting laughter, and I am captivated by the loud singing by the fire, desperate to join in to fill my head with joyful songs and noise. One step, two steps, my sandals slide across the damp grass as I dodge between locked-lip lovers, stumbling drunks, and an intimate group of friends smoking pot in a circle, inhaling their natural high. I secretly inhale as I pass by.

Weaving between the trail of littered beer cans and the procession of stumbling drunks, I turn as one amateur drinker grabs me to balance himself. Unable to avoid his swerving, I am knocked off base.

"Jerk, get a grip." I instinctively push him away, sending him on his wobbly path.

The uneven earth below my sandals sends me in my own downward direction. My jacket is knocked off my shoulders and lands on the trampled path behind me. The crisp, chill air sweeps across my bare shoulders, and my forward fall is unstoppable. Flailing, arms swinging, contorting my crouching body, I swiftly reach way back to sweep the jacket up off the muddied grass.

Glancing back, I see more drunken feet approaching fast. Hurrying, teetering on my toes, I touch the ground for balance and try to regain stability to stand.

Out of the midnight sky, a hand of rescue presents itself to me. I grab it like a sponge, my fingers interlacing in the soft fibers. The tender grip swiftly pulls me up, ending my out-of-control balancing act. Someone holds on tenderly and briskly moves my disheveled body off to the side to safety.

Embarrassed and winded, my vision blurred in the smoky darkness, I squint to filter out the bright bonfire light to see who has come to my salvation.

Blindly I speak into the darkness and say, "Thank you."

Stepping closer, words escape me. It is him. Heaven is standing in front of me. *Sister, I am eating the apple.*

He hands me his beer cup, gracefully walks behind me, and places my jacket back over my shoulders. Leaning in from behind, his body pressing firmly into mine, he whispers in my ear, "Hi, I'm Adam. I think I just saved you. I'm like Superman."

Motionless, taking in his beauty as he steps around to stand in front of me, I feel the heat of his hands still resonating in mine. My voice cracks as I clear my throat, trying to say my name. Still holding his beer cup, my quivering lips grip the rim and let the cool frost coat my throat. Slowly moving my tongue across my top lip, swallowing hard, I clear my throat again.

"Hello. Thank you, Superman. You saved me from the sea of drunks. I hope you are not one of them." Then smiling I say, "My name is Jules, and I'm more of a Spiderman kind of girl."

"Jules," he says. "I was coming over to tell you we have a date tomorrow night, but you disappeared off into the fire pit."

I answer with hesitation in my voice. "We do? I don't even know you. You look familiar though, just can't place it yet. Did my softball team send you over? Are you looking for a terrible pitcher?"

"No, but are you a terrible pitcher?"

"Is this a joke?"

"No, why?"

"Well, on occasion I have been. You sure this isn't a setup?"

"I'm sure. That's why we have a date, so you can figure out where you know me from and hopefully never forget me."

"Hmm, never forget you in a good way or a bad way?"

"You will find that out." Leaning over, he whispers in my ear, "Be ready tomorrow night at five p.m. Wear running shoes. I hope you are a runner. If you are not one now, you are going to be one."

His heavenly body draws me in like a magnet, pulling me closer, sealing the natural connection between us, melting us together like glue.

Looking up into his eyes I say, "Running shoes will be on and ready at six p.m."

His fingertips glide over my palms. Smiling, he intertwines our fingers, pushing my chin up with his other hand. He looks down and his eyes meet mine. Shivers radiate throughout my whole body. His warm hand moves to my shoulders. He pulls me close and says, "I want to look into those blue eyes forever."

His words warm my heart, my soul. Is this what love at first sight feels like? He lifts me off the ground, and his strong embrace encases all my fears, worries, and doubts and grinds them into dust. My face warms with happiness and I smile.

"Every story has an ending," he says. "I hope ours never does."

Okay. Sister, this is what I was talking about: love.

Smiling up at him, I know this feels right.

"Come, I want you to meet my friends." He grabs my hand, and we make our way toward his group of friends, swimming through the sea of partiers.

CHAPTER THREE

The phone is ringing. I dance down the hallway to get to the singing tone, swing around the kitchen wall, and skid to a stop. I casually pick up the phone on the third ring.

Deep breath in, clear my throat. "Hello." I listen. "Yes, this is Jules. Hi, Adam. See you in a bit. Yes, that's the address — brick house, number 3890. Bye."

One, two, three steps, twirling down the plush green carpeting, I dance back to my room so I can look one more time in the full-length mirror. I check my hair, smoothing down the flyaway loose strands. I bite my lower lip to stop it from trembling. My heart beats faster, pounding beneath my athletic bra. I reach up to tighten my ponytail, pulling too hard, to calm my nerves.

Why did I agree to this? Then again, I can always run away from him. I chuckle. The sound of his car door slamming makes my skin tingle. It's happening — my running date is here.

I sprint to the front door and swing open the screen, watching my date's strong, muscular legs work their way up the sidewalk.

"That was quick. You must live close by," I say, my eyes dancing in pleasure.

"Yes, I will show you where I live next time."

Next time? There is already a next time?

"Are you ready? You look so cute," he says.

"Where are we going?"

"I was thinking a short run through the Metro Park first, followed by a little after-run snack in the meadow. I brought a blanket and drinks. Are you game for that?" He smiles down at me, and I take in his sweet smell — it seeps deep into my pores.

I look away, embarrassed by my behavior, not recognizing my own self.

"Sounds great. I should warn you, I hold the record for the mile in my age group. I hope you can keep up with me!"

I push the screen door open and jump down the stairs off the front porch, stretching my arms above my head as I walk down the sidewalk to his car.

I glance back and watch him jogging out the door to catch up. I cover my mouth with my hand, hiding my gigantic smile, a snickering giggle escaping my lips. Do I tell him now or later that record was in fifth grade? Later!

&. &. &.

The wind whispers through the treetops, rejuvenating my perspiring body. Moving rapidly in unison, we sprint forward on the trail. As our feet hit the blanketed pine-needle forest floor, we take in the sounds only a runner becomes accustomed to. We weave between giant pines and majestic maple trees, passing mile marker two. I let out a deep breath. Sunlight filters through the festive treetops, which are painted with oranges and fiery reds.

"It is so quiet and beautiful. The leaves are starting to change so early this year," I say, trying not to sound too winded.

"One more mile and we will end up at the field where we parked the car. Do you need to stop?" he asks with no sign of breathlessness.

"Me? Stop? Nope. Never. First one to touch the car wins."

Sprinting ahead with a burst of bundled-up happiness, I pound the trail, rolling freely. The final stretch lies before me. The car is in sight, the prize ahead of me, but the sound of Adam's shoes crushing the leaves is getting nearer with each stride as he closes the gap between us.

I need a plan to slow him down. Slowing my gait, I yell back to him, "Adam, I need to tell you something."

"Now?" He stops, jogging in place. The heat from his body radiates to mine.

"Yes, now." I'm winded and try to catch my breath.

Looking up into his beautiful brown eyes, I frame his sweaty cheeks with my hands and say, "I had a really great time today."

"That's what you had to tell me. Is the date over?"

"No, I had to tell you this."

Tipping up on my toes, I place my lips on his, barely touching. A sigh escapes from deep within me.

Surprising me, he urgently presses his lips to mine, parting my lips. Our tongues magically touch, slow dancing together.

Pulling away I say, "Wow, that was amazing. I want to do that again. But not now—I have a race to win."

I take off down the trail, leaving him standing there speechless. Head down, I pump my arms, my feet pulsating with painful pleasure. I turn to see where my competition is. He is still standing in awe, feet planted, looking in my direction.

"And one more thing, Adam. I am very competitive."

"Oh, I see how this is going to be. Let me tell you something, Jules. So am I." His leg muscles bulge as he sprints toward me to close the gap once more. Breathing heavily, I gasp for air and lunge forward, my arms stretched ahead, inches between me and the car. Bam, his arms are wrapped tightly around my waist. Swinging my feet into the air, he twirls my body away from the finish line. Our bodies are deliciously tight, and I inhale his steamy, sweet sweat as it combines with mine. I close my eyes and forget about the finish line, enjoying the feel of his hands on my body.

We are teetering off balance, our bodies gratifyingly tangled. His body crashes down in the grassy field, pulling me along. I topple onto him, giggling with pleasure, and lie hidden in the flowing field of yellow soft petals, muttering, "Cheater!"

"Me a cheater? You are the one who smacked that kiss on me. It took my breath away," he says.

His lips come toward mine before I can respond.

"Mmm." Moans of pleasure come from my mouth, and I enjoy this slow and unhurried second kiss.

And then it hits me. My eyes flash open. I know where I have seen him.

Sister, is this how you are going to get me back to church?

Pulling my lips from his, I say, "Oh my God. You are an altar boy at Saint Anthony's Catholic Church!"

"How did you know? From my kiss?" He chuckles.

"Absolutely. I would know it anywhere — the altar boy kiss." *Sister, you got me good.*

CHAPTER FOUR

Junior year has begun. The trees stand bare, their leaves drifting in every direction the wind will take them. Winter looms closer, bringing a chill to the air when I get out of bed in the morning. The one thing that isn't cold is my heart. It's smitten with a beautiful boy who fills me with wonder, holds me tenderly, and inspires me to accept any challenge. His charm, his words, the tenderness of his magical touch, work their way deeper into my heart. Our endless weekend nights are spent together at parties, movies with friends, or quiet time for just the two of us in my basement. As we cuddle on the couch, his body secretly talks to mine with a simple touch or gentle rub of his fingers on my skin. The TV is on but muted by our unforced laughter and conversation.

"Want to see me dance?" he asks.

"You said you don't dance."

"I don't, but I will do anything for you. Will you be my date to the Christmas formal?"

Jumping on top of him, I straddle his body, rubbing my hands up and down his chest over his T-shirt. I capture his ab muscles beneath my fingertips, answering in more ways than one.

"Yes, yes, yes. I want to see you dance and yes, for me, there will always only be you for every dance, date, life."

Adam is one year older than I am. His body is fit and strong, his mind full of knowledge and big dreams. Our conversations are boundless; his dreams of success are over the top. His words fill my mind with wonder and a desire to know all I can about what's in his mind and how deep his heart can feel.

"But we have so many other things to look forward to," I say.

"I love your blue eyes."

"Don't try to distract me with flattery. But it is my favorite color," I say, tickling him along his rib cage.

"Jules, that tickles. I'm very ticklish," he says, trying to push my hand away. "See, we have so much in common. I love your blue eyes, and it's your favorite color."

"Adam, that makes no sense whatsoever."

My fingers jump back on his stomach. "Ticklish, hmm." The joy of hearing his infectious laugh makes me yearn for more. Giggling erupts into a belly laugh and wrestling.

"Tell me something else I don't know about you," he says.

"I don't like raw onions."

"Grilled?"

"Yes, love grilled."

"Hmm, me too."

"Where do you want to live when we are old, like twenty-five?" A smile covers my face.

"Florida. Somewhere warm for sure. Sun and sand and — " He grabs me, holds me in his grip, and our bodies sink deeper into the worn cushions. "Anywhere that I can kiss you anytime I want!"

"The sun, sand, ocean-blue waters all are on my list. Hmm, but not sure Florida is the answer for me. You can still kiss me anytime you want."

Tipping my head back, I close my eyes, inhaling his glorious scent. His soft lips touch mine. Rhythmic music plays in my head, which brings a calm to my body. Bound to each other by our unspoken words, we melt into the harmony of a song I never want to end.

🐝 🐝 🐝

The driveway is dusted with the cool flakes of winter's white sparklers. He's here. The car slowly comes up the driveway, the tires crunching the snow beneath them, car tracks melting the snowflakes below. The car door slams shut. I love that sound. Adam is here.

Running back to my room, I take one last glance at my red dress in the mirror. The soft satin bounds snuggly down my body. A smile spreads across my face. I'm happy in love. My heart pounds faster with visions of Adam in his black tux. Swirling, twirling around one more time, I stop in front of the mirror and throw my head back, feeling a dart of unexpected pleasure. I gently grab my dress above the knee, lifting the edges off the ground, and point my toe and glide my foot into my black suede high heels. I swing my gold heart necklace around my neck as my other hand lifts my hair out of the way and I secure the clasp. Making a final check in the mirror, I slip on my shiny hoop earrings.

Christmas lights brighten the living room, casting shadows on the walls. The Christmas tree fills the air with the smell of pine. I run down the hall, and lifting my dress, I hop onto the couch to look out the big picture window. I pull the curtains apart and my heart slows to a calm pace watching him saunter down the sidewalk to my front door. Adam sees me and a big smile illuminates his face. His smile makes me smile. I jump off the couch and run to the front door. I swing it open, letting in the winter chill. He bends down, and his cool lips touch mine. Closing my eyes, I touch my warm lips to his, taking a slow inhale of his aromatic cologne.

He grabs both my hands and moves me out of the doorway. His sultry eyes move musically up my body, starting at my shoes. Yards of red satin cling to my slight curves. My gold heart necklace hangs seamlessly; my gold hoop earrings hide beneath long curled locks of blond hair. His fingers pulsate in my hand as his eyes finish with a gaze into my own. He grips me tighter as he pulls my body closer to him with one swift tug. Unsteady on my heels, I rest my head on his chest in calm pleasure.

His breath is warm on my skin. Dropping my hands, he wraps his arms around me and whispers, "You are beautiful in that red dress. You drive me crazy."

Reaching down, he hands me my corsage box. I flip the box open, and he slides the corsage onto my wrist. The three bundled red roses, blanketed in baby's breath, gently tied with a white satin ribbon, tie our evening wear together: a bookend couple.

"Jules and Adam, stand in front of the Christmas tree so I can take some pictures," Mom says, appearing out of the kitchen with a camera in her hand.

"Just a few, Mom. We are going to Adam's for more pictures."

Adam nods his head in acknowledgment.

Leaning into him, I say, "By the way, you look irresistibly handsome in that tux tonight."

With my eyes zeroing in on him, my hands graze over his chest as I pretend to straighten his vest. I tug on the edges of his bow tie before we both swing around, smiling for our photo shoot by the tree.

"Smile." Click, click, click. The flash momentarily blinds our vision.

Adam grabs my hand. "Good night, Mrs. Kane. I will have her home in the morning after the dance breakfast."

"Bye, Mom, love you. Tell Dad sorry I missed him before he got home from work."

Music fills the Holiday Inn banquet room with holiday cheer. Flowing gowns and rented tuxes already fill the dance floor. The disco ball throws sparkles around the walls. Bodies rock in unison. The disc jockey is playing "All I Want for Christmas." The smell of pine fills the room from the dozen or more decorated Christmas trees that surround the party room.

Fingers intertwined like a woven mat, we enter the room.

"Jules, there they are, over there. They saved us a spot at the table."

I follow behind him as we weave our way around the tables to reach our spot.

"Hurry, put your coat and purse down. I want to get this over with."

"Get what over with?

"I like this song. Let's dance."

Pulling me onto the dance floor, he works his way through the crowd, cocooning us in the middle so no one will see him.

"May I have this dance and keep my promise that I would?" He does the cha-cha around me comically, his arms flying above his head.

"Get over here, you weirdo. This is a slow song. Wrap that luscious body around mine and dip me over your knee, John Travolta."

"Oh, the dance moves are going to come out now, my beauty."

When I place my head on his shoulder, our bodies become one, and we sway to the slow music. He holds me close, and nothing can distract me from this unselfish love.

"All I want for Christmas is you, too," he sings in my ear.

"I knew you could dance."

"I can dance; I just don't like to. But I would do anything for you."

The slow song ends, and the beat picks up with a hell-raising song. Dropping my hands from his neck, I sway my hands over my head, shuffling my feet side to side.

"Ah no, Jules, my body is not going to move like that, and if it did, it would not look pretty." He turns to walk away.

Giggling and following behind, I grab his waist to form a caboose on the train leaving the dance floor and kick side to side from beneath my dress as we head back to the table.

Our friends gather around, and the loud laughter eases down a few decibels as we nibble on food in the buffet line, eating between picture taking and group dancing. I return to the table sweaty and playful to find Adam waiting for me.

I collapse into the chair next to him, and he tucks the loose locks of hair behind my ear — it's tousled from rocking to the beat on the dance floor with my girlfriends. Drinks splashed on the dance floor and the loose meatball from dinner that missed my mouth leave my red satin dress dotted with stains. My feet pulsate like beating drums from high-heel torture. Thank goodness that was the last song.

The principal appears on the stage and the lights go on. "Ladies and gentlemen, thank you, everyone, for a successful 1979 Christmas Formal. Drive safe and Merry Christmas."

Teens scramble, gathering purses filled with lip gloss, shoes tossed under tables, ties and cummerbunds in arrays of colors — blues, reds, greens — thrown over chair backs. They yelp and holler to find their dates to hustle off to the after-party.

"See you at my house for the after-hours party," Billy announces to everyone at the table.

Adam squeezes my hand. "You okay with that?"

"I go where you go." He brings my hand to his lips.

Billy's house is a short drive down Interstate 77 to Mildred Street. It's the same house where Adam and I met at the end-of-summer party.

"Hello, we're here."

"Come in, Adam. Since when do you knock?" she says.

We are not the first to arrive. Two couples are already intertwined on two extra-long couches, the dark-brown carpeted floor covered with sleeping bags. Two more couples double up on armchairs in the large family room. Constant chatter fills the room, everyone talking above everyone else, telling stories about the evening's highlights. High-heeled shoes are kicked to the corners; cummerbunds are once again sprawled over backs of chairs. Adam and I settle in for the night, and I kick off my shoes.

No one can leave if they have anything to drink.

"I'll be right back. I packed some things in the car for us."

Adam heads back out the door and reappears a few minutes later with a backpack thrown over his shoulder, blanket and pillows clutched under his arms. Dropping his backpack, he spreads out the blanket in front of the fireplace and fluffs the pillows, making a cozy, romantic spot to rest our dancing queen bodies.

"Aw, Adam, you are so good to me."

He swoops me up and carries me over to the blanket, lowering me down gently. He reaches into his backpack for two beers. After opening one, he hands it down to me and snuggles in behind me, allowing my back to rest against his chest. My body molds to his like clay, and I feel his heartbeat slow to match mine.

After popping open his beer, he holds it in front of me and says, "To us, to the moon and back, I love you."

My heart lifts in my chest. "May we always be together under the sun and moon. Adam, I love you too."

CHAPTER FIVE

Adam is a senior now. Every chance we get, we talk about what we will do when he goes off to college next year and about our future together. It has me on edge, but he comforts me with promises of a future with us intertwined into eternity. His applications are in, and now our lives hang in the balance. I will finish up my last year of high school. No matter which school he goes to, we can write and call, and he will be home for breaks. We will always be together, bound by an unexplained connection.

Cuddling on the couch, our bodies close, his hands comfort me with his velvety touch, softly gliding over my shoulders, down my arms, to find my hand. Rubbing his thumb round and round on my palm, he murmurs, "Touching, just being by your side calms me, calms my worries, my fears, and makes me happy."

"My eyes are going to close," I whisper, my lids growing heavy. "So tired. I want to fall asleep in your arms and wake up in your dreams."

His answer thrills me. "Jules, you are my dream come true."

Still, I'm cautious. "You say that now, but . . ."

"Listen to me. I'll be with you on the phone, with you by mail, with you when I come home. You'll barely know I'm gone," Adam says, nuzzling against me.

It's going to be okay. He wants me. He'll wait for me. My senior year will go by in a flash. I'll focus on school, make good grades, get myself ready for him. It'll be as though he never left. It has to be. My eyes flutter, and I drift off to sleep, secure in my dreams.

𐅋 𐅋 𐅋

The months fly by. Adam talks of us moving to Florida after college, complete with runs on the beach, stargazing under the moonlit sky, and picnics under the setting sun. Our dream is alive. I love him; he loves me. Comfortable and comforting, this is going to be an easy forever and ever. I only imagine my life with him. He is my life, and together we are perfection. His touch, his smile, and his love make me happy. Making him happy makes me even happier. *Sister, this is the love I was talking about.*

Lulled into love's stupor, I'm not prepared for what comes next. He's accepted. Adam will be going away to college, to Harvard, the oldest institution of higher learning. Harvard, so far away from me. Ten hours too far. Graduation is getting closer, just as fast as the late spring sunlight hits my face earlier in the mornings. The sun warms my face; Adam warms my heart.

The reality of separation whirls in my head.

"Adam, what happens next?" I ask, a little breathless. "You're leaving for college. Will there still be room for me in your life?"

"Shh." He rubs circles on my back. "We have all summer. We have forever, and forever is not long enough for me," he tells me.

"It's ten hours, Adam. Ten hours and thirty-three minutes by car." If I even had a car.

"We'll work it out. We always work stuff out. This will be no different," he says.

I turn toward him, look into his eyes. "Wherever you are, you know I will be right here waiting for you."

"I love you." He kisses me on the nose. "Now stop worrying. We have six weeks of school and all summer together before I leave for college."

"That's why I love you. You have it all figured out."

⸙ ⸙ ⸙

"Mom, if you go to the store today, can you buy me some tampons?"

"I thought I just did, but I will stop sometime today."

"Gotta go, Mom. See you after practice," I say, running out the garage door to catch the bus.

My monthly nightmare of a period is on its thirteenth straight day. Heavy cramping and continual bleeding convince my brain I am either dying or teenage menstrual cycles suck.

Mom notices my drawn pale face. And she notices the bathroom trash can full of bloodied tampons and unsightly soaked pads; her snide comments let me know it. Night after night, when I get home from practice, I drag my lethargic zombie body down the hallway to my room, the sun still high in the sky. I skip dinner, my eyelids heavy with the anticipation of sleep, my body tortured by the muscle cramps blindsiding me into unconsciousness. Dozing off, I hear a faint knock on the door. Mom enters.

"I made a doctor's appointment for you tomorrow after practice. You need to get a checkup. Your period is way too long and heavy," she says.

"Okay, thanks, Mom." Nodding her way, I roll over.

Next afternoon, I see Mom's car approaching, punctual as usual. Practice is winding down. I shovel the rest of my equipment into my baseball bag, and I trot toward her car. It stops, and I open the back door and toss my bag into the backseat, then hop into the front.

"Hi, Mom. I'm starving."

"I came straight from the restaurant. Do I smell like grilled onions? How was practice? Tell the doctor about your periods."

"Mom, stop."

"Did you pitch today? Your period, it's been going on for weeks. Don't forget to tell him that. The bathroom garbage can is a mess."

"Yes, Mom, I pitched today, and you always smell like onions and hamburgers! It makes me hungry. Did you bring me a burger?"

"Your father needs help at the restaurant but won't hire anyone, and you need to empty the wastebasket occasionally. Your father doesn't like to see that bloody mess. Your burger is in the backseat." She digs in her purse for her lipstick.

After she parks, I open the door and head into the doctor's office ahead of her. As I approach the check-in window, the receptionist slides the little privacy window open to greet me.

"Hi, appointment for Jules Kane."

She hands me a clipboard with some forms to fill out, and I turn to take my seat as Mom walks in. We wait awkwardly in the empty doctor's office. I look for something to read, spreading out the magazines like a fan on the table. It's *Readers Digest* or *Highlights*. Minutes later, the door opens. I see a familiar face as Nurse Sharon calls out to the empty waiting room.

"Juliette."

I chuckle to myself. Hello. We are the only ones here. I have been coming here since I was born or, no, wait — since before I was born.

"I guess that would be me, Sharon. And please not Juliette. Jules, Sharon, please! Remember, Romeo and Juliette."

As I step through the doorway, the laces from my rubber cleats drag along the floor. I head to the only examining room and jump up on the table. I look around the room — not much has changed in the seventeen years I've been coming here. The red barn picture with rolling green fields hangs slightly off kilter against the baby blue accent wall.

The nurse closes the door, then sits on the desk chair and rolls closer to me.

"So, Jules, why are you here today?" Nurse Sharon asks over her reading glasses, which sit low on her nose.

"Day fourteen or fifteen of my period, and it's heavy bleeding, tampon plus a pad. No appetite, tired. Did I say tired already?" The nurse scribbles fast on my open chart. "Tired, I sleep twelve hours some days."

"Any pain? Stomach?" she asks without looking up.

"Just the normal cramps I get every time I get my period."

She closes my folder, grabs the thermometer off the wall, and shoves it into my mouth. Then she grabs my hand, putting pressure on my wrist while listening through the stethoscope.

"No fever, blood pressure normal. The doctor will be right in. He hasn't seen you in a while. He'll be surprised how grown-up you are. Nice to see you, Jules." She puts my folder on the outside of the door and quickly closes it behind her before I can answer back, Nice to see you too, Sharon.

A few seconds later, there's a quick knock on the door and Dr. Bronski enters. This is the doctor who delivered me into my mother's arms seventeen years ago. I have been seeing him since I was . . . *Lifetime* is the number I say to myself. He looks old, with sunken brown eyes, a balding head, and curly gray sprouts hovering above each ear.

"Hi, Jules." He smiles. "What's bothering you today, and why am I honored with a visit from you? Your chart says you have had your period for an extended time. Right?"

"Yes."

"Any other symptoms? Tired?"

"Yes."

"How is your appetite?"

"Haven't really noticed a change."

"It is baseball season. I see you are still playing." He points to my outfit. "Still pitching?"

"Yes, still trying to pitch," I say.

"Are you overdoing it? Is that a possibility? Let's look, and then we will talk some more. Open wide, Jules."

He slides the tongue depressor into my mouth, and I gag from the pressure on my tongue. As he examines my throat, Dr. Bronski requests ohs and ahs from me. Moving my head to the right, then the left, he tugs on my earlobes, pushes my chin up as I roll my eyes to the ceiling. His cool fingertips press on my stomach, probing along to the other side. Gently gliding his large-palmed hand behind my shoulders, he helps me sit up on the examining table. When he taps on my kneecap, my foot pops up, reacting on cue. He listens with his stethoscope for the beat of my heart as I take big breaths in and out. His breath matches mine with each inhale and exhale.

Stepping back, he hesitates for a few long seconds before he speaks.

"Anything else you want to tell me?" he says.

I shake my head side to side. "No, nothing I can think of."

"Okay, then," he says. "Go home, rest, maybe take tomorrow off from all activity. Get caught up. It could be you are overdoing it with softball, school, and not enough rest on the weekends. I am writing you a prescription for the pill to help control your heavy menstrual cycle, but first we need to monitor this period. Hopefully it will stop any day and you can start on the pill next Monday. If it hasn't stopped by next Monday, you call and come back in. We can do some blood work and look at other options and test for mono."

He rips the prescription off his pad and hands it over to me as he advances to the door. Then he stops and pivots, looking directly at me with a prolonged gaze. I wait for an explanation. Is it a diagnosis? Does he want to tell me something more? I want to yell, Tell me. Am I sick? Dying?

I watch, waiting for his lips to move and words to form, but his head drops. He places his hands in the pockets of his white doctor coat and says, "I hope you'll face your obstacles and go on to succeed in your future. Follow your dreams, Jules." He opens the door and steps out, closing it behind him. I can hear his footsteps disappearing down the tile hallway.

Wait . . . what? I sit in silence listening to my deep breathing, processing his words. Shaking my head, confused, I jump off the table, open the door, and look for him right and then left down the hallway. He is nowhere in sight. I push open the exit door into the waiting room. Mom looks up, but I walk through the office, out the door, and straight to the car. I stand with my arms crossed against my chest, my thoughts weighted as I lean against the car, the heat from the car fusing into my body.

Mom rushes to catch up with me. She starts the car, turning to see if anything is behind her. "What did the doctor say?" she asks as she puts the car in reverse.

"I'm fine, just need rest. He wants me to see him next week if my period hasn't let up by then."

"Okay, I can leave work early if you need me to."

"He gave me a prescription for birth control." Flipping the piece of paper between my fingers, I wait for her reaction, but she keeps her eyes straight ahead on the road, hands firmly planted on the steering wheel.

Leaning my head against the car window, I notice the sun throwing my reflection back at me. I pray that one of us can figure this out as I stare at my twin shadow.

"Mom, can I drive to school tomorrow? That way I can drop my prescription off after school. The pharmacy is closed now. It's past seven." Say yes, please. It's her day off. Say yes. My eyes close in silent prayer.

"Hmm, I suppose."

"Thanks," I whisper into the window. Drained physically, I'm emotionally crippled with questions. Isn't the doctor supposed to make you feel better? Again, I ponder the reasons for his last words to me. Am I sick and he didn't want to tell me? The car pulls into the garage. The day's events are jumbled in my head. I sit trancelike, my mind deep in thought.

"Jules. We're home. Don't forget your bag in the backseat." Mom gets out, slamming the door behind her.

I lumber into the house, shuffling down the carpeted hall to my room, and close the door behind me. With no strength to take all my clothes off, I sit on my bed and kick off my shoes. Rolling my sweaty, stinky socks into a ball, I throw them toward my hamper. As I crumple into bed, unfolding under my covers, I unwrap all the questions that need answers.

CHAPTER SIX

M y eyes open to the jagged blare of my alarm, and my hand reaches over to quash the rude awakening. The clock reads 6:00 a.m. Twelve hours of sleep under my toasty comforter. I should feel rested. I stretch my tight muscles toward the ceiling before jumping out of bed and heading to the shower. Water washes away my night sweat, but the doctor's words weigh heavily, replaying again and again in my mind. He was telling me something. What was it? If I am dying, I am going to school to see Adam. He is my light in the darkness.

"Bye, Mom, I'm leaving. I have practice tonight, and afterward I am going to watch Adam's cross-country meet." Scrambling quickly through the house and juggling my books and locker bag, I open the door out to the garage. It slams closed behind me. Whew, I avoided Mom. My day is stacked too full to take a day off from school. I have morning weight training and evening practice. If I miss any of those required practices, I don't play in Friday's game.

Crossing paths with Adam in the hallway, I feel the gentle slide of his hand in mine, a kiss on my lips, and then we hurry in opposite directions to our next class.

"I will try to meet you at your cross-country track meet today," I yell down the hallway after him. "Run fast."

He waves back, a big smile on his face, blowing kisses in my direction and says, "See you at the finish line."

After school, I change in the locker room and walk out to the fields for practice. I drag myself through batting practice, then the twenty minutes of base running has me feeling weak in the legs and light-headed. I grab my mitt, and with my cleated feet pounding the dirt, I make my way over to my pitching coach.

"Hey, Coach, do you mind if I cut out a few minutes early? I'm not feeling so hot."

"Sure, Jules. Why didn't you tell me this morning at weight training?" Coach says, shaking her head at me.

"Because I want to play Friday."

"Go, get out of here. Drink some water. You look pale."

"Will do. Thanks."

Flashing a big wave goodbye toward my teammates still on the field, I make my way to the car. My teammates, who are finishing up on the field, return the signal with flair. Checking my watch, I notice the cross-country track meet doesn't end for another hour, leaving me time before Adam crosses the finish line. Before I start my birth control pills, I need to do one more thing. Something has been knocking on my brain. That look on the doctor's face has left me with questions.

Driving extra miles to avoid a familiar face or family friend, I cruise through neighboring towns and pull into the Ralphs Grocery and Pharmacy parking lot. I park far away from the entrance and grab the steering wheel with both hands, the sun blinding my eyes with the reflection off the car hood. Still in my practice gear, I sprint through the store's front door and pace the aisles, my knees nervously knocking together. I stop when I read the sign for Feminine Needs and search the shelves for my "needs."

"Can I help you find something today?" a voice pops out from behind me.

Startled, I jump to attention. "No. Thanks."

My fingers tremble when I grab the first pregnancy test box I see. Shoving the box under my baggy softball jersey sleeve, I zigzag my way to the checkout stand.

Revealing my cargo, I place it on the black grocery belt. The belt moves; I move. I hover over my precious merchandise. The belt stops; I stop.

Shirley stands behind the checkout counter. My eyes focus on her name tag. My mouth is frozen shut, teeth chattering like birds in a tree.

"Will that be all?" she asks.

"Yes." Are you fricking kidding me? I'm not buying a candy bar.

"Total is nine dollars and forty-three cents, miss," Shirley says, with a slightly tilted head and a neutral expression.

Slowly uncurling my tightly fisted sweaty palm, my crumpled money emerges, hot, right out of the oven. I unroll the steaming ten-dollar bill and hand it over to Shirley. Our eyes meet. I look for judgment in her eyes. A sympathetic smile fills her face, her sunken eyes talking to me with empathy. Has she been in my shoes before? Smiling back, I appreciate her kindness. She places my change in my glistening palm. I grab my bag of truths and head out, counting my steps as I walk to the door.

My pace is steady and fast. I walk right past the car, cross the parking lot, and head for the restroom at the neighboring TGIF restaurant. Nervously I chuckle, sweat forming in my sports bra. What day is it? I ask myself. It's Friday, thank God. I enter, pause, and scan the restaurant for the restroom sign. I beeline right for it. Pushing through the bathroom door, I stop and stare at myself in the mirror. I am an imposter in someone else's story. My body hangs low; I check for shoes below the bathroom stall doors. I swing open the door of a vacant one and hurriedly lock it behind me. Unsure of what to do next, I check the lock again. I slowly lower myself onto the toilet seat, open the box, and tear open the instructions. Through blurred vision, I speed-read, concentrating on the bold highlights.

I fixate on the written words and stick figure people on the page. Step One. Pull out the stick, open packaging. "No shit," I say aloud. Step Two. Remove cap. Step Three. Sit on toilet and urinate a steady flow on the stick. I maneuver my softball pants off, the stick harbored in my hand. I sit back down. I check my watch for the start time. I sit and observe the cold metal beige walls as the pressure of my bladder is released. Step Four. Try not to stare at the stick during the duration of the waiting period; you will become more anxious. I blurt out, "Go fuck yourself, step four."

My ears are my guardian, guarding my piece of real estate as the bathroom door opens and footsteps tap across the floor. I check my lock again. The door to the stall next to me swings open, then closes and locks. I peer under to see black patent leather pumps. More movement, flush, footsteps, water on, water off, the paper towel dispenser clicks, and I imagine the towel presenting itself to my guest as she looks in the mirror. Door opens and closes. Silence. I relax, alone again.

My feet are planted flat. I glare at the stick as it lies cradled in my palms and close my eyes for one last prayer, hoping Sister Elizabeth can't hear. Dear God, I call to you in signs of trouble because you answer my prayers. Please, please help me. Help us.

My foot taps at high speed on the cold bathroom floor. Sixty more seconds: one, one thousand; two, one thousand; three, one thousand; ten, one thousand. I lose count, and the numbers jump in my head. I count faster and faster. I jump to forty, one thousand; fifty, one thousand. Sixty seconds of life pass by. My chest hurts. I choke back several final breaths as I start to hyperventilate. I know I can't be pregnant. I have my period now and never missed a period. But I just need to be sure. One eye opens. My eyelashes filter the light worming in. I'm squinting as my cheeks rise. Both eyes barely open, I flip the stick over. My body plunges forward, the air sucked from my lungs as my chest crashes onto my knees. I slouch over, my chest flares, I hold my breath. I wrap my arms around my knees, head hung heavy between my legs as my cleats shriek forward on the tile floor. The test stick slips through my trembling fingers, smacking the tile floor. Teardrops well in my eyes. My eyes burn like fire. I am pregnant with Adam's baby.

🐌 🐌 🐌

Flushing the evidence, I watch as the water swirls around like a tornado, gaining speed. My stomach churns, and bile builds in my throat. I can't be pregnant. My period? We have been responsible . . . except, oh, God help me, that one night. Cuddling on a blanket, peering up at the clear moonlit sky, lucent stars sparkling back at us . . .

"Jules, look there." Adam's finger pointed in the darkness.

"Sirius, or Dog Star, brightest star in the night sky."

"You serious?" I joked back, giggling.

Ignoring my silliness, he continued, "Jupiter, Saturn, Mars, and Venus." The excitement in his voice made these clusters of planets dance in the sky.

Passion got the best of us. He put his hands on my body, unable to resist the urge, the urgency of showing our love. This gorgeous creature held me, the one love who had no intention of restricting my spirit but let it run free and embraced it.

Pulling away, I said, "Adam, we shouldn't."

"Yes, you are right." He removed his warm hands from my heated body.

My lips touched his. "You are my world. Thank you for loving me," I said, relieved he understood.

My fingertips glossed tenderly down his back. The warm, familiar touch on his body reignited us both. There was no turning back from the strong rhythms. *Sister, I gave my heart, my soul, all of me to him that day, until death do us part and our story ends.*

That must have been the night. Clasping my hands together, I bring them to my heart. Frustrated with my weakness, I know we should have waited that night. My stomach whirls again. I'm not regretting what I shared with him, but I am regretting we can't take it back and do it right.

Warm bile rising in my throat, bitterness floats in my mouth. I stand and wiggle my softball pants up over my hips. Turning just in time, the contents of my stomach empty into the toilet, acknowledgment that my life is forcefully exploding.

My face is hot and moist, and sweat drips inside my bra. I wipe my mouth before unlocking the stall door. Digging deep to find some energy, I drag my leaden feet out of the women's restroom and enter the outside world a changed person. My gaze travels up to the vast blue skies above, and I pray to the higher horizons. God, do you see me? I am now a pregnant teenager, in love with the altar boy, wearing a softball uniform, of all things. My hand rises to my abdomen, gently rubbing my newfound companion. What are we going to do now? Walking briskly to my car, I pause before I get in. I throw my tormented body up against the car door. I squint up to the heavens looking for answers. Because all I have is questions.

❦ ❦ ❦

My fingers tremble as I try to unlock the car. When I slide behind the wheel, autopilot takes over my movements. I drive through the streets with muddied thoughts and a desire to flee, to vanish among the living and start over. Maybe I should just keep driving. The music is loud, louder than usual. My ears ring from the drumming bass of an unfamiliar song. I push the radio buttons, one after another, in search of escape. Can someone please play a love song? Finally, belting out the lyrics on the radio, I search for answers between the words.

I drive back into my town, seeing familiar street signs, and park in a secluded space in the meadow park far away from humanity. I turn the car off, and the sudden silence is stifling, suffocating me and now my baby, so I roll the window down for air, inhaling deeply to save us both.

In the distance, a crowd gathers at the finish line; the high school cross-country race is coming to the end. The first runners sporadically appear out of the woods, their track shoes pounding the path, following the ribbon-lined route, making their final push to the finish line, trying to close the tight gaps between them. Adam leads the group. His muscular legs carry him the distance, and he crosses the finish line only seconds before his competitors, securing first place. Beaming, I bring my hands to my chest and inhale deeply. Seeing him temporarily comforts me, but then the smile is wiped from my face by the vision of the beating heart in my squeamish stomach. The sudden urge to retch hangs in my throat.

Sister Elizabeth, I do not know everything at the age of seventeen. I am lost in a grown-up world. Two teenagers having a child was not the plan. My future is off course. Flashing back to my doctor's appointment, did Dr. Bronski know I was pregnant? Was he trying to tell me? When he said, "I hope you'll face your obstacles and go on to succeed. Follow your dreams," was this what he meant?

Sitting in the car, unable to move to congratulate my winner, I roll the window down, inhaling the fresh perfumed blooms in the spring air. Budding wildflowers of crisp yellows fill the slopes. The cross-country meet is over; the runners disperse to their cars. Adam sees my car and jogs toward me, his smile matching his great accomplishment.

"Hi. I am so happy to see you. Why did you park here?" he says, leaning in the window.

Arms folded, resting on the car door, he plants a sweaty kiss on my cheek. Sweat from running fifteen miles flows down his face. Swiftly, he wipes it away from his face and mine.

Shock shears away his smile the moment he sees he is not only wiping away his sweat but also the tears pouring down my face. I'm wanting to run, flee fifteen miles away. I squeeze my eyes shut to stop the flow; drool forms at the corners of my mouth.

"Jules, what is wrong?" His voice is soft and gentle.

My silence is his killer. Frustrated, Adam walks around and gets in the passenger side of the car. Confused by my silence, he stares at me, his face draped in worry. Urgently he grabs my hands, placing them between his sweaty palms.

He pleads again, "Jules, talk to me. Did something happen?"

I ask, "Do you love me?" I choke back tears, and my chin hits my chest. I sniff and wipe my runny nose with my sleeve.

"Yes, of course I love you."

Exhaling in relief, I pull back and look directly at him. "Our love is about to be tested," I whisper. "I'm pregnant."

Silent in this moment of despair, we sit numb, staring straight ahead, digesting the reality of a baby.

"Are you sure? How do you know?" Shooting off questions, Adam crumbles forward in the seat, his hands covering his face.

"I went to the doctor, but he didn't tell me. I think he wanted to tell me. I don't know, Adam." Pausing, I sigh heavily. "I am just as confused as you." My shoulders inch up toward my ears. "I've had my period for over two weeks. I don't know, Adam. How could this happen to us?"

"What are you going to do?" He shakes his head. "I'm sorry, what are we going to do?"

"A baby, us, now?" I babble out loud.

"I'm going away to college in the fall." He pauses for a while. "I can find somewhere closer," he says at last.

I bite my lip. "That's your dream." My arms collapse over the steering wheel. "This is where we had our first date," I say, peering out over the flower-covered field.

"That was a wonderful day," is all he says. Now on this spring day, spring brings new growth — we have our own new seed. Our lives are taking us down an unknown path. Which path do we choose, or do we even have a choice? No longer two of us in the picture — it has grown to three.

He swallows and his hand feels cold in mine. "We need to tell our parents," Adam says, his voice cracking a little.

Sister, I kissed the altar boy and got pregnant. Can you call my mother and tell her?

CHAPTER SEVEN

Light peeks through the window, but I close my eyes to the sun of the day. Fatigue bangs on my head as I try to ignore the events to come. I lie face-down on my bed, arms cradling my head to ease my heartache. I anticipate Adam's arrival — my knight, my miracle — and imagine that, somehow, I escape this trial. The house is quiet. A black cloud lowered in and brought dead air. No one is talking to me since I told them I was pregnant. Adam is on his way to my house with his parents to discuss this shattering news.

My body tenses when I hear the ring of the door-bell. The high-pitched chime vibrates down to the bone. The bell that brings answers? Change? Resolution? Motionless, I wait and listen. Footsteps approach the front door, the screen door squeaks when it opens and slams shut as our guests are welcomed. Feet shuffle around as if dancing on the tile entrance floor.

My heart is crashing. A wave of fear barrels over my head, and I'm filled with doubt. I am acting cowardly; I need to face this storm. Throwing the covers to the side, I try to decipher the mumbled chatter.

Chairs slide back and forth across the linoleum floor as everyone gathers around the family dining room table. Family table seems so ironic.

I need to pull myself together and join them. I push my dead weight off the bed, and I throw my shoulders back as my feet hit the floor. I stand tall and shake off the chill that's blowing in from the other room. Fear is all that faces me, and I will face it. I walk down the hallway, the plush green carpeting silencing my sinful entrance. The smell of freshly brewed coffee makes my stomach churn as I enter the kitchen. I glance down at the meeting table. Everyone clings to their coffee cups, which remain in their saucers. A serving platter at the center of the table displays an assortment of delicate pastries. I say under my breath, "This is not a party, Mom!" This party has started — without me. Slowly I traipse around the dining table, stalking the guests. I stare at the offerings my mother has displayed. I consider just circling the table again and again, corralling them in, but I do a half circle and slide into the snack-bar stool next to Adam, swiveling it around to face the conversation. He reaches down to hold my hand.

Flowered wallpaper surrounds the dining room. I stare at the repetitive pattern of soft pink carnations with dark green leaves, the long stems interlaced by a bow. Flashbacks of my grandfather's funeral fill my thoughts. The carnation on his lapel as he lies in his open coffin, smiling up at me.

High on the ceiling, the gold-rimmed crystal chandelier spews light from each teardrop crystal. Dancing specks of light and shining stars sprinkle across the room. As I fade in and out of the conversation about our schooling, our futures, our reputations, the light entrances me. I watch lips move in conversation.

"What if she keeps the baby?"

What IF? I am waiting for the two Catholic families to mention church or the teachings of Sister Mary Elizabeth.

Oddly today, as we all sit at the last supper drinking coffee and eating Danish, no one is blessing the food. Are we not Catholic today? Secrets and lies are as bright as the reflection spinning off the sparkling chandelier. Still drowning, I'm trying to stay afloat, listening with ears full of water. Mumbled talk about me surrounds me.

"We have to think about her reputation."

My reputation? What about Adam's? Is there a double standard here? I didn't do this to myself. My name is not Mary.

"Adam is already accepted and going away to college this fall," his mother says.

What will happen to me? I sit in silence, gasp for air, the water too high for me to breathe. In my head I yell, I can hear you, I am right here. I rock back and forth in my seat, building up momentum for the courage to say what I think. I want to keep this baby, Adam's baby. Rocking deeper into the water, sloshing in my seat, I cross my arms over my small bundle, cover my not-so-virgin ears, blocking the voices, shutting out the hatred and selfishness in this imitation prayer group. My heart aches, the water floods in. I can't stay afloat; I am drowning in this conversation because my words are silenced.

"Our only option is for her to not have this baby." Heads nod around the table.

"And end this pregnancy as soon as possible."

"It's best for everyone." Yeses are whispered in prayer voices.

Ocean waters fill my eye sockets; tears wallop and the wave crashes down on the rocky shore. Droplets cascade down my cheeks.

"We can all move on, like it never happened," Mom says as she steps away from the table. "I have some names of clinics. I've already made some phone calls to get information. I'll call to confirm."

Hearing their words, I gasp for air. Adam squeezes my hand harder. Tears roll down my face, but I don't bother to erase them — I want this table before me to see my aching heart. I place Adam's hand on my stomach as tears fall for the heartbeat inside of me; they are the only things real in this room.

He leans closer and whispers into my ear, "I wish I could kiss us away from here. I adore you."

A muffled whimper escapes from deep in my chest. Nodding my head up and down, I say, "Me too."

The table rattles and shakes as everyone pushes their chairs abruptly away. Everyone is standing, except for Dad. He sits alone, his elbows on the table, fingertips pressed into his forehead, holding not only his head but, I have a feeling, also his heart. My gentle giant in distress, my own apostle — shattered; he has procreated a sinner.

Mom returns to the table. Their plan to change fate and eliminate one human life has been set in motion. "Tomorrow we will drive to the Women's Healthy Choices Clinic in Detroit," she says.

Quickly I calculate the date of the planned assassination: May 2, 1980. No one can say the word "abortion" because it is not the Catholic Church way. Dad pushes his chair from underneath him and stands with dignity, reenacting exactly how I feel. The wind has been taken from my sail; I see a hazy horizon. Hurriedly he wipes away the tear that has dropped overboard. My anchor gathers me in his arms, tugging at my heart to keep me afloat.

Sister Mary Elizabeth taught me to "Do unto others as you would have them do unto you." The Golden Rule, love our enemies. Am I the enemy?

Suddenly I envision church on a Sunday. The giant entrance doors are open and welcoming. Welcoming to whom? Gays, lesbians, divorcees, baby killers? Will you all stroll in, heads held high, bathe in holy water, parade to the front pew, kneel and pray in the name of the Father, the Son, and the Holy Spirit? Will they pray for the sinner? Will my altar boy stand by the priest who offers forgiveness of sin through communion? Who exactly is the sinner?

Adam looks back as his parents usher him to the front door. His mom leads the charge to escape from my house. Our eyes stay locked until his mother pauses, leans into him, leans closer, her lips firm, her words quick and quiet in his ear. Instantly his body sags, his eyes appear somber, the air has been taken out of him. His shoulders cave. He grabs the door handle, and she breezes past him out the door. Before he walks out he looks back at me briefly, then leaves, closing the door behind him. What did she say? I run to the door, pressing my forehead against the solid wood. On my tiptoes, I look out the small glass window, watching him walk away. My voice is a whisper. "Stay with me — you are all I need."

I stand alone. The evening's events ignite shock waves down my legs. Teetering, I lean forward, forcing my feet to follow. The oversized chair is within inches. My legs ache from supporting my strong façade, my body spins, and I sink deep into the cushioned seat. I rest my hands on my belly, rubbing circles over my only comrade. I gaze back to the kitchen, to the flowered wallpaper blooming on the kitchen walls. The funeral service has started for my unborn, and I imagine the organ music echoing over and over. All my guests have retreated to living their lives, leaving me alone. My soul cleaves to the dust they left behind for me to clean up.

CHAPTER EIGHT

Retreating to my room, I lie coffin-like in bed, holding on to the silence with my powder-blue sheet pulled high over my head as night closes in on me. Filling my lungs is laborious, and I wish each breath were my last. I pray to any God that will listen. Afraid, I can't close my eyes. The clock counts the seconds, tick, tick, ticking in my head, each minute bringing me closer to the early morning hours. A chill fills my bones like dew covers the grass.

A car door slams in the dark. Adam is here. Rolling out of my casket, I plant my feet on the floor and run. My toes crush into the plush carpeting as I race down the hallway. I swing open the door leading to the garage and press the opener — the giant door methodically retracts into the ceiling. As the door rises, I gradually see his feet, his jeans, his waist, and finally all of him. Mom blazes past me. She heads to the drop-off car idling in the driveway. What is she doing? Why does she need to talk to them? It's 4:00 a.m. Our appointment is four hours away. He walks through the garage and up the steps that lead into the well-lit kitchen. His eyes focus on me, his only friend in this house. Jumping into him, I frantically place my head on his chest. He holds me close, tenderly kissing the top of my head. I grasp him tighter, rocking back and forth, closing my eyes.

The angry voltage of my mother's voice pierces my eardrums. "Jules, get in the car," Mom yells from the cold garage. Startled, the crispness in her voice separates us, and we escape in the morning darkness to the garage. Four car doors open and slam shut. The criminals of love sit in the back, judges in the front. Dad behind the wheel, Mom settled in the passenger seat. Adam and I sit in separate cells in the backseat like scolded lovers.

Mom passes an envelope over the seat to Adam. "Adam, this is for you." She never turns to look him in the eyes. He reaches up and grabs it. His eyebrows crease and he looks at me. I can't solve this mystery.

She says, "This is money for your ticket home from Detroit today. You will not be coming home with us. You will be taking a bus back, and your parents will pick you up at the bus station in town."

"No." I shake my head, repulsed at the idea. "I want Adam with me."

She slowly turns to meet my gaze. "What you want no longer matters."

The big green sign reads North I-77 to Detroit, the on-ramp with no U-turn. We enter the freeway. The car is quiet; the car is cold. The fan on the heater blows double-time to warm the car's temperature, but not the passengers' temperaments. I stretch my hand across the seat, palm up, and he instantly knows what I need: consoling. Intertwining his fingers with mine, he confirms that our story is forever just ours. Slowly he turns his head toward me. Our eyes meet, our hearts bound to each other's; we will not be pulled apart. I throw myself across the car seat, and he wraps his arms around me, not caring what the judges in the front seat think. For three hours, we hold each other, dozing in and out of restless sleep, bound, unbreakable, family for one last time. No words spoken, only three hearts beating as one as the car races to the funeral.

Dad exits the freeway. The car comes to a complete stop at the top of the ramp. My heart beats faster. He looks left, looks right. I want to ask, "Are we almost there?" But I don't want to know the answer, so I don't move or talk. We drive at a pace car rate, slow and steady, for a few more minutes. The race is over. The car slows to a crawl and into a parking lot as Dad scans the address numbers on the buildings. The parking lot is early dawn dark and empty, a few cars parked sporadically here and there.

"This is it," Dad says.

"You two, get out. We will meet you inside in a bit," Mom coolly demands.

Adam opens his car door and hops out, pulling me with him. My feet hit the blacktop, balancing my weighted sin. We walk as one toward the red brick building.

Adam shivers, exhaling the cold morning air. "It's going to be all right."

He squeezes my hand, and we cross through the double glass doors. The smell of bleach and the bright white walls prompt my sluggish eyes to open. Scanning the waiting room with teary eyes, I notice we are not alone. *Sister, could there be more sinners?*

We approach the desk to find a large woman in baby-blue scrubs sitting behind it. The color accents her eyes; a stethoscope hangs from her neck. She looks up and says, "Sign in and take a seat."

Together we walk across the room, Adam pulling me like I am in a drunken stupor, guiding me to sit on a wooden bench along the window. My teeth chatter, and I rock side to side, trying to find comfort in the grains of wood beneath my thighs.

How did I get here? Panic washes over my body, my mind racing as I listen to the muffled whispers. The front door opens and closes. I see the exit, a getaway. Should I run, run to save my baby? Scooting my heavy body to the front of my seat, I imagine grabbing Adam's hand and running hand in hand out those doors, sailing right past Mom, to freedom. I sit, shivering, blocking out the silence. How did this happen? *Sister, what lesson am I supposed to learn today?*

ॐ ॐ ॐ

I hear the rattle of the chair wheels rolling across the floor, and my senses go on full alert. There is movement behind the desk. The splashing shadow on the wall gets larger, the silhouette dark and smoky. The mystery figure appears from behind the wall and stares intently at the pages on the clipboard resting on her forearm. She is holding a pen between her fingers, twirling it as she shifts her gum cheek to cheek with an intermittent chew. She begins to speak; her mouth is moving. I watch her lips pucker to form the sound of a J. Her voice pushing out the words takes my breath away. "Next. Juliette Kane." My stomach aches, tears are brewing; little sips of air hold them back. *Sister, can I sit in silence? Juliette is not here — ask Sister Elizabeth.*

I stare at Adam. Drooping slightly forward, he stares back at me. Our intertwined fingers clutch harder, turning our knuckles white. I hold on to my lifeline, squeezing even more tightly, petitioning to a higher God. Call his name. Call Adam's name, too! Make him stand, walk with me. Walk across this room of shame. Stand with me, for me, for us.

She calls my name again. "Juliette Kane."

Standing statue erect, I lock my knees to stop the shaking panic going on inside me. My feet shuffle on the floor. I move one step toward the voice, our hands slipping apart, the fabric holding us together slowly unraveling.

I whisper, "I love you, just love me."

"I do love you, my blue-eyed girl."

My heart is on the floor as I move my feet closer toward the voice. I stretch my hand out to him, tears rolling down my cheeks. Grab my hand, pull me back, take me to Florida. Blocking out the voice barking in my ear, "Juliette, this way please."

"We are going up to the fourth floor, if you need to tell anyone," my escort says.

"I told Sister Elizabeth. No one else needs to know."

My soldier body is numb as I stand in front of the elevator. The cold metal doors show my reflection: one reflection. I am alone; no one will know I am on the fourth floor. Slowly turning, I stare across the square-tiled floor to the front-door entrance. I watch my parents walking through the double doors of the building. They walk to the information desk. Words are exchanged, and they turn and wave to Adam. Adam gets up, walks toward them, never turning again to look at me. He nervously obeys and slithers behind them. I take two slow steps into the elevator, numb with silence. She pushes the number four. The doors are closing me in, and my palms sweat with panic. I jump out and watch him walk away from me, out the front door, two steps behind Mom and Dad. *Sister, can I take the bus home, too?*

Dazed and alone, feeling deserted, I trail behind, following the nurse down the hollow hallway, looking for some kindness on the faces passing by me. We stop halfway down the hall. The door to Room 7 is open. Four beds, equally spaced, line the room. I'm the first guest to arrive. We stop at the first bed by the door. She hurriedly grabs the curtain—swish goes the fabric to seal me in.

"Juliette, this is your bed." Sorry, Juliette is not here. Opening the cabinet doors, she pulls out a gown, tossing it on the bed. "Here is a gown. Take all your clothes off and put them in this basket. Do you have any valuables?"

"No valuables." I plop down hard on the hospital bed, rattling the railings holding it together.

Swoosh goes the curtain again. "Great, change out of your clothes and I will be back."

Blood pumping into my heart, my pulse races. Nausea sets in, and only rapid swallowing curbs the urge to throw up. Kicking off my shoes, I hop on the bed and take small sips of water, trying to settle my stomach, listening to the whispers in the hallway.

Who else is on the fourth floor? Other girls—women who have their own story to tell—are they sitting alone with no one to tell it to? Hurriedly, I strip down, sliding my arms through the armholes, tying the gown blindly behind me. White crisp sheets below me, I lie in this dimly lit room, curtains closed to block the impending sunlight of the new day rising.

Swoosh goes the privacy curtain; the wind chills me. So much for privacy. Who has startled me by entering my own private hell?

"Take this, it will help with pain later," the nurse says. "Your turn is next. We will be taking you in for your procedure." A small paper pill cup is placed in front of my face. I toss them into my mouth. One big gulp of water chases the reliever of all pain. Swoosh goes the curtain. Closed.

"It's not working. I am still in pain," I yell past the curtain, the words echoing off the walls.

Pain — the pain of what is to come — is a killer. I want my heart to stop beating, just like it will for my temporary guest inside of me — the one guest everyone wants to check out early. Yet the nurse acts like this is something to look forward to: my turn. Footsteps follow the squeaky wheelchair rolling on the tile floor, the sound parroting off the wall. I listen for the squeak to stop and the footsteps to quiet themselves at my curtained-off room. Is it my turn? Do you want to console me before it's my turn? But the footsteps disappear.

The demon sounds in these halls fill me with fear. The moaning, the crying, have me curious. Is anyone offering soothing words, condolences to those crying out?

Contacting the only God I know, I look for comfort, grasping my hands in prayer position. God, please hear my voice between these four walls of hell. What was my penance the Father gave me at my last confession? Five Hail Marys, five Our Fathers, hmm, could have been ten. Oh hail, I can't remember. How about I start with one?

"Hail Mary, full of Marcella. Our Lord is with thee. Blessed art thou among women and blessed is the fruit of my . . . Holy shit!" pierces through my lips.

Blindsided, my joints stiffen from the bolting pain forcefully infused into my groin, sharp knives twisting torture in my stomach. My mouth drops open as I gasp for relief, inhaling short breaths while the knives carve around to my lower back.

Kicking frantically, shuffling my legs back and forth, I punt the crisp white sheet off my body, freeing my legs from the crumpled knot tangled in my bed. I swing my legs over the edge and drop my feet to the floor. Grabbing the bed railing for balance, one hand, two hands, my knuckles whiten. The pain builds again. Gripping tighter this time around the cold metal pole, like a rope climber, I try to lift myself up. Legs unsteady, my knees wavering beneath me, I fall back onto the bed, the knife-wrenching pain crippling deep to the core one more time, exploding fireworks in my spine.

My vision blurs like watercolors. A water glass multiplies on my side table, and I try to reach for one of them. My hand shakes. I'm unsure which one is real, so I guess, knocking the water glass to the floor.

My mouth drops wide open. I wait for the high-pitched scream to escape my lips, the identical one that is screaming through my body. It's quiet. Sweat drips down the side of my face, connecting with the tears streaming from my eyes. My hospital gown is drenched, draping over my paralyzed cadaver-like body.

A shallow whisper, "Help me," escapes my lips. "Help me," I murmur the words again.

The silent calm haunts me.

The pain builds inside me, sweat drips off the tip of my nose, and I anticipate a repeat of what just happened. Gasping for a reprieve, I dig my finger-nails into my drenched hospital gown and look down at the floor, aghast at the pool of blood below me, red lava cascading down my legs. The red pool widens on the white tile floor, my ruby slippers overflowing. What is happening? A fresh storm brews and builds. Lightning strikes, electric bolts twist across my groin, the storm tossing my body in every direction. My body is stricken on overload and my head, violently thrown back, dangles over the edge as my feet sway just above the floor. Drenched hair fans across my face; heavy eyes roll back, resting in their sockets. Bile builds in my mouth, and my head rolls to the side. No longer able to mask the pain, my body collapses at the murder scene.

 🐾 🐾 🐾

My mind is quiet; my eyelids weighted. I try to block out the voices vibrating off the darkness. I look straight into the light. *Sister, is that you calling me? Should I follow the light?*

Who is calling my name?

"J-U-L-I-E-T-T-E, Jules . . . Do you hear me?"

Sister?

I lie still in the hospital bed, lips slightly parted, air whistling in and out. I am a crucifix lying in my own bloodbath.

"Get her back in bed. We need help in Room 7," muffled voices yell.

My mind swirls in confusion. Heavy footsteps surround me, garbled words float past me. Room 7,
that's my room.

"Grab her legs."

"She has lost a lot of blood. She delivered."

"Check her vitals."

What? It's over? My eyes open wide, the harsh
glare of the fluorescent lights blinding me. As I fight
the fog, shadowy figures circle all around my bed.

🐚 🐚 🐚

One of the nurses is cradling something; she has my
gown. It's now ruby red. She is wrapping it in a towel.

Is that my cherub? I lift my hand, my bloodied
fingertips barely reaching toward her. My silent cries
for consolation go unnoticed as she turns and walks
out the door. I raise my right hand in the name of
the Father, the Son, and the Holy Spirit, marking
the sin in blood across my body.

Swoosh goes the curtain.

🐚 🐚 🐚

"Time to go. Get up and get dressed."

A thin layer of sweat covers my body, and my hair
is strewn across my face. Voices rumble in my brain,
which is trying to make sense of the words.

"What?"

"Time to go home," she says.

"What time is it? How long have I been sleeping?"

"It's 4:15. My shift started at three. You've been sleeping since I showed up," the nurse tells me. "Your parents are waiting in the lobby. Take this." A cup of water and two capsules appear before my eyes. Not knowing, not caring what they are, hoping for cyanide, I toss them into my mouth like a grenade waiting for the detonation.

She reaches under my bed and places my clothes on the end. "Time to get dressed," she says. Swoosh goes the curtain.

☙ ☙ ☙

Was it sweat or tears on my cheeks that woke me again? It's all a blur since the last swish of the curtain. The back of my hand grazes over my face to move the tamped-down hair off my damp cheeks. Lifting my head, I discover I'm curled up in the backseat of the car. I see the back of Dad's head in the driver's seat. I am headed home, rocking myself back and forth, breathing heavily through the gut-wrenching timed cramps. My damp breath is hot on my skin. No one to hold me, I hold myself. Lost in my journey, confused by the last hours, I'm helplessly alone to battle the demons in my head.

Adam, I need you. I am not the only sinner, I repeat to myself. I didn't do this alone. Ask me and I will tell you! One problem solved, many more have just been created.

CHAPTER NINE

The hairline crack in the ceiling reminds me where I am. My headphones are tucked tight in my ears. Music blares to muffle my pain. "Call me, call me, Adam, call me! I need you now," I whisper. Clasping my hands together in prayer position, I add, "Hear this, God. Bless me, Father, for I have sinned, or so they say. Amen."

I roll over and dangle my legs off the bed. In the darkness, I reach over to the nightstand, moving my hand back and forth along the edges of its square surface, touching each corner as I search for my telephone. I need someone to talk to. I need to talk to Adam. I search along the floor for the cord, check the phone jack in the wall, and discover my phone is missing. Where is my phone? Why is it not here? Sitting up, I switch on the light, and I look at the orange shag carpet behind the nightstand, focusing on the abandoned phone jack.

"Mom," I scream out, "where is my phone? I want my fucking phone."

My heart beats faster, and I slither up the bed to look again behind the nightstand. How is Adam going to call me? How is he going to take me away from here if he can't call me?

"Mom, I know you can hear me. I want my phone." My voice gets weaker, my trembling lips whisper, "I need someone to talk to."

Footsteps approach my darkened sanctuary, getting louder, like horses' hooves. I roll over to face the wall, hugging my pillow, and throw the heavy comforter over my halo head. I close my eyes, pretending to sleep.

The door opens and Mom takes two steps in, her hand resting on the door handle, twisting it back and forth.

"You are forbidden from calling him. I have removed the temptation — you will not see him or talk to him."

Though I try to tune her out, my lips quiver with anger. The squeaky, twisting doorknob rattles my nerves even more.

"Mom, stop," I yell into my pillow, my body heat rising.

"He does not want to see you or talk to you. Do you hear me, Jules?"

"Did he tell you that on the way to the bus? What did you say to him?"

"He used you, Jules. Don't let it happen again. Don't go out and get pregnant again!"

The squeaking stops. The prison door closes.

I squeeze my eyes shut, closing off her verbal abuse, blocking her voice, her gouging words that keep replaying. To occupy my brain, I repeat his phone number over and over in my head. I will never forget it, and she is wrong: he loves me. I roll over and face the closed door. My voice quivers with hate, and as I choke back vengeance, saliva fills my mouth. I'm yelling and spit splatters back on my chin. "I hate you. I hate this house. I will leave. I will escape this hell. And you are wrong — he does love me."

The walls shake and my vision blurs from the vibrating voices and slamming doors. Where is Adam? Why is he not coming to me? I am missing him; I am missing a part of me.

Reaching across my body, I swoop up the pill bottle and, with a firm grip, I press down, pushing and twisting to break the childproof lock. I stifle my snide chuckle. Childproof my ass. Click, click, click — the tamperproof bottle opens. I shake a handful of painkillers into my palm. Picking one up from the pile, I roll the round edge between my fingertips and toss the pill into my mouth.

Temptation haunts me, my fingertip circles each smooth edge, around and around. Pushing them side to side, separating two, plus two more, sliding ten more off to the side. The water glass prances on the table, glistening in its place. I peer down at permanent salvation in my grip.

Take them. Water, pills. Water, pills. My thoughts rattle with the sarcasm of crushed dreams of love.

Sister, do I want to live long enough to find the love I told you about? Or am I the fool to believe it exists?

Four walls close in around me; tears fill my eyes with doubt.

Cupping my hand, I form a funnel, slowly shoveling the white painkillers back into the bottle, twisting the tempting cap closed.

I will leave . . . walk out of this house one way, one day, but not today in a body bag.

Today my escape is only temporary. Reaching for my water glass, I let water flow into my mouth, swishing it around, dissolving the sulfate residue on my tongue. The chalky paste follows the dissolving painkiller as it slides off my tongue down the back of my throat.

The real escape will come; the noose around my neck will loosen. I just don't know when. Circling the room, mentally taking pictures for my memory bank, I trace the small ceiling crack with my finger in the air. As my head falls back against the pillow, I pull my knees up tight to my chest, wrapping my arms around them, rocking back and forth, cradling myself with comfort.

I will be true to my words, I promise you that, Sister. The lids of my eyes heavy, the weight of my depression slowly creeps in. I fall back into my darkness, the noose hanging loosely around my neck.

❧ ❧ ❧

Must be a different morning, I think as I reach over and try to wrap myself around him. I find nothing but cold sweat on the empty sheet next to me. My bedroom doorknob turns and the door creeps open. Slowly opening my eyes, my face planted deep in my pillow, my arms over my head, I wait. Wait for the words of the day.

"Juliette, get up, get up. Stop feeling sorry for yourself."

"What did you say, Mom?"

"You did this to yourself. I hope you don't do it again!"

I lie there silent, a string of thoughts flowing through my brain. What did I do, Mom? Fall in love? Don't worry, it's only my heart that's suffering — the price of love is costly.

My silent voice gains strength, my broken heart crumbling inside. The rumbling in my brain unleashes and I yell, "Leave me alone." Spit spews from between my trembling lips when the words leave my mouth. "Bring me my phone so I can get the fuck out of here." The door slams behind her to silence me.

Prisoner in my own house — no phone, no one to call, no Adam. What is she telling my friends who call? I'm busy? Busy doing what? Busy trying to figure out a reason to stay alive. Water cup and two capsules before me, I grab them, throwing them into my mouth like a grenade. Boom! Out go the lights.

Days roll into nights. I wipe the sweat and tears from my face and remain confined in my solitude, wallowing in what has happened. Adam hasn't come to visit me. The void he's left adds to my feelings of desertion.

The early morning darkness is silent and peaceful as the earth cools itself from the warm spring day before. It's 4:00 a.m. I listen through the open window for the morning sounds that will block the shallow beat of my heart. The dark, smoky sky mimics the dark thoughts running through my head. Why didn't I say no, I want to keep my baby? I drift off again.

Startled by the roughness of the loud voice, I squint to shield the light.

Mom is standing over me. "Wake up, Jules. Get up."

Back and forth I rock like a cradle. Her hands grip deeper into my skin, trying to wake me.

"Get dressed. You have a counseling appointment at four. It's two o'clock in the afternoon." She pulls the window curtain open.

"Get up, for God's sake. Go get some help so this doesn't happen again."

Shaking my head in confusion, I roll over to face her. "So what doesn't happen again?" I ask.

"Get pregnant." The words flow easily from her mouth. She turns, walks out the door, shuts it behind her.

I am afraid to speak, knowing my thoughts are dark and cloudy. The hurt she has inflicted on me seems to momentarily take the air from my lungs. My mouth stays closed, and I silence my voice, disengaging from her hurtful words. I stagger out of bed, my body weak, wobbling across the room. My eyes are half-closed, shielding out the daylight. I drop my sweat-drenched T-shirt and pants onto the floor. I drag my hand across the carpeted floor in search of clean clothes and head for the car.

As I drive myself away from hell, the freedom feels refreshing. I turn the car radio on, twisting the knob until music fills the silent void. Louder and louder it plays to drown out the dangerous thoughts of this solo rider. My foot eases off the gas pedal to slow. It's time away for good behavior, I think, laughing to myself as the car glides to a stop at the red light. The fresh air slowly brings regenerated life into my lungs, the new air energizing me to counsel the counselor.

I strut out of the car, toss the keys in the air, and catch them in one swipe. I wrestle with the hair knotted in my undone ponytail and slick the greasy, unbrushed mess behind my ear. I straighten my wrinkled attire: crumpled Rolling Stones T-shirt and blue drawstring sweatpants. I climb up the stairs two by two, and my flip-flops slap the concrete steps to the fifth floor. Flippantly clipping down the hallway to Room 502, I swing open the door to an empty office, exhale in relief, and walk straight for the unmanned desk. I read the instructions: 1) Print and sign your complete name. 2) Flip the green switch on the wall when you are ready. A vase with daisy-decorated pens rests next to the sign-in sheet. I grab a daisy pen — the tip grinds into the paper as the ink spells out my name. First name: Juliette. Middle: I pause with my pen as a smile comes across my face. Pen hits the paper with more vengeance.

Elizabeth. Last Name: Kane. Juliette Elizabeth Kane. Laughing out loud, I put the flower-topped pen back in the garden pot holder. Smiling feels good. I flip the green switch on the wall, flop into the seat by the door, slouching in the cushioned office chair.

Unladylike, I sit in my unladylike outfit. I tap my foot, counting the empty chairs in the room to occupy my mind. My tapping distracts me from the depressing elevator music that plays softly through the speakers. The mellow melody makes me anxious. How about some upbeat music here, folks?

My mind rehearses what I'm going to say. I am here for help — unburden me of my sins. I go over possible questions she is going to ask me. "So, Jules . . . your mom has told me you seem withdrawn, unmotivated, and lie in your dark room listening to music?" Answer my own question . . . hmm, could I be depressed? You are fucking kidding me. I know I'm depressed! I lay screaming in a dark room by myself and delivered a dead baby.

A woman opens the door. Making eye contact, we exchange a cordial smile while she walks over to the sign-in sheet.

I stand up and straighten my wrinkled T-shirt. I might be a little underdressed. I roll my eyes. My foot rocks from heel to toe with each step, my flip-flops slapping across the floor. Stopping at the doorway, I meet her gaze and say, "Call me Jules."

"Okay, Jules it is. Have a seat wherever looks comfortable."

Scanning my new surroundings, I walk straight for the gray leather chair. The cool leather feels good. Legs together, hands in my lap, I crisscross my fingers in prayer position and observe her awards of achievement displayed across the wall. I search for sunlight from the big glass windows and watch the gentle breeze wrestling through the trees. Will I have plaques and awards like that someday? She makes her way to her wing-backed leather chair. On top of the side table next to it is a notebook — the notebook of answers, I assume.

I shift in the leather seat, waiting in silence for the first question.

"Let me tell you about myself before I ask you to tell me about yourself," she says. "I have a PhD in clinical psychology and have been practicing in the area for six years. Feel free to ask me questions anytime. You can do the talking, or I am here to help with engaging us in conversation." She picks up her notebook and a pen. "Everything we say here is confidential and between us. So let's talk. Would you like to tell me about yourself, Jules?"

With a shrug, I allow my body to sink against the smooth leather of the chair.

"I understand we need to find a place to start over in your life. Let's call it a new beginning."

I smile, then I let out a chuckle. My stomach moves in laughter. "Hmm, interesting. Who said I need a new beginning?

"Your mom mentioned — "

"Let me stop you there." I look her in the eye. "Here's the thing. I got pregnant, was persuaded to have an abortion — it was best for me, us, I was told — I'm not so sure now. My mom calls me 'easy.' My phone, my friends, and the one person I love have been taken from me." I pause and her expression remains annoyingly neutral. "So why do you think I am here? Never mind. I will tell you why I am here. Because once again, I have no choice."

She sighs. "Your mom is worried this may happen again."

Blood surges through my veins, my pulse racing to catch up. My mouth drops open. "Oh, really?" I say, rolling my eyes. I lick my dry lips, gazing down at my blue sweatpants that I picked up off the floor only minutes before.

"Reality is, I haven't washed my hair, come to think of it, or showered, in five, six, maybe seven days. I can't really tell you exactly when because I don't even know what day it is right now."

Using my fingers, I comb my disheveled, greasy hair away from my face.

"I cannot tell you when soap or water rained upon this sex symbol of a body." I pucker my upper lip, sliding my tongue over my front teeth, confirming a toothbrush did not touch these sandpaper teeth today. "I didn't even brush my teeth today, counselor." Pausing, I inhale deeply. "So I am confident, no, one hundred percent sure this party girl is not going to stop and have sex on the way home today."

"Jules, I just need to explore and understand your feelings."

"My feelings — funny — no one seemed to care before. The only thing anyone cares about is this secret. Are you here to help me? Because I think I am doing a better job of surviving on my own."

I drop my stare to the square-patterned carpeting, tune out the speech, and all I hear is muted mumbling flowing from her mouth. I lift my eyes, meeting her midsentence.

". . . you need to respect yourself for others to respect you," she preaches.

The clock says 4:49 p.m. The second hand moves at precision pace. To kill time, I repeat numbers in my head — Adam's phone number — over and over in my head.

"Jules, are you listening?"

Awakening me from my phone dialing, she stands. "Our time is up for today. What a great start."

Time is up, perfect timing. Adam doesn't seem to be answering. My mind hangs up the phone. I stand and walk out the door. From behind, I hear her. "See you next session, Jules."

๑ ๑ ๑

I hustle up the stairs — nervous energy fuels the effort — anxious to get started with my session. I sign in: Juliette Elizabeth Kane. Switch the toggle to green, indicating my arrival. Immediately the door opens and she waves me in.

Walking directly to the couch, I flop my sexy body dressed in sweatpants and a T-shirt in the middle and wait for the first question. She settles into her wing-backed leather chair. Beyond the big glass windows, the trees sway in the wind. I sense her gaze in my peripheral vision, so I wait.

"How was your week, Jules?" She breaks the silence.

"Good," I reply.

"Did you go to school?"

"Yes."

"How was that?"

I continue responding with one-word sentences. "Okay."

"Have you been socializing?"

"What does that mean?"

"Have you been going out? Are you interested in anything new?"

"Like?"

"Clubs? Group activities?"

"No."

"Are you interested in having sex again?"

I turn to look at her. What is she talking about?

"Have you slept with anyone else since the abortion?"

Flashing back to catechism, I plead the fifth, unwilling to engage in insults or defend myself for loving someone, for making love with one person, my soul mate, my sweetest devotion. My stomach retracts; my ribs spasm from the torture to my heart. Fire travels upward, hitting my cheeks.

"Hmm, I didn't make any plans to sleep with anyone else. Let me think, school, home, school, home . . . nope, haven't slept with anyone. I was thinking of being a lesbian. Would that be okay with my mom?" Fire shoots from my eyes, aimed straight at her.

"Because this love thing, loving a man with your whole heart, loving him forever thing didn't seem to work for me!"

She says, "We can save that for another session."

"You sure? We can talk about it now if you want to." In that split second, I know I am never coming back here. "This session is over. I'm over. Done!"

I stand, controlling the urge to cartwheel my way out of her office—the grand finale.

Lesson learned today: I will take care of myself.

Her words echo down the hall. "Good session, Jules. See you next time."

I push the door open to the stairway, and I jump two steps at a time down the emergency fire escape. As I push open the heavy metal door to freedom, the sound of alarms goes off behind me. I saved myself, my own emergency escape. This sinner vows to never be silenced again. *Sister, I failed myself and my baby once—it will never happen again. Sister Elizabeth, I just told the counselor I'm considering being a lesbian. What do you think about that lie?*

Laughter erupts from deep in my stomach as I envision the Sister's face registering those words in catechism, the black-and-white habit pinching her face tighter, anger filling her ruby-red cheeks.

I imagine her walking to her desk, opening the top drawer. Out comes the ruler, followed by, "Juliette, there will be no more outbursts or you will be in the hall."

Careful, Sister, I might like that ruler tapping on my body. My stomach hurts from laughter, and tears roll down my cheeks. *Sister, Sister, don't get mad. Love one another, right? I think I've climaxed at the mere thought of it.* Throwing my head back, I wipe my dirty laughing tears with the sleeve of my T-shirt.

CHAPTER TEN

I've managed to drag myself to school for the last three weeks. I quit the softball team and can't remember what I told the coach. It didn't really matter. Nothing matters.

Adam doesn't talk to me at school. He passes me in the halls with heavy eyes that never reach mine. The darkness of my sadness shadows me. My breath is shallow, and I quiet my panicking heart at the sound of his voice. Faint in the knees, I see him in the distance and freeze at a standstill. What happened to our unconditional love, kissing me any time you wanted, forever? Here I stand, broken, the pieces lie around me, shattered into a million slices. His eyes are set straight ahead as he forges on by me, never stopping to pick up any piece of me.

He keeps walking, walks right into his future, and graduates, finishing his senior year without me. Mom was right—he is selfish and used me. *I will pray for him, Sister. Will you pray for him too? Maybe he can find his soul?*

Fog has settled into my brain. Since the abortion, it seems like I am no longer processing memories. I travel through daily life in a slow-paced trance with no memory of the last day of school. The days end in my bed, alone.

Summer parties continue night after night. My friends invite me, and sometimes I go, but there's nothing memorable enough to remember. Graduation celebrations, barbecues, teeth brushing, showers are all a blur . . . it could have been the painkillers, loneliness, depression, or the trauma of my whole life — a life scrapped for garbage. A new beginning is what the counselor told me I needed. I cannot start a new beginning because it, too, will have an ending. I can't take another ending right now.

I still remember those Saturday morning teachings in catechism. I need to forget those. I still remember the teachings at Sunday Mass, meaningless preached words, now useless. I still remember my planned future with someone I loved — scratch those. Maybe real love doesn't exist. Our love story that was never going to end? It ended. Adam, why did you end it and write a new ending — the forever ending?

My friends share information about Adam in hopes we will get back together. It was a shocking overnight breakup, not just for me. No one can figure out why we are no longer together. Adam and I have a secret. A carnal sin that will go to my grave, mine alone. I don't know what he will do with his secret. I never had the opportunity to ask.

I don't say much about the breakup because I don't understand it either. I stopped being his girlfriend overnight. The mere mention of his name throws my whole body into collapse, and I shut down. I stop listening when they talk of him. My brain stops my heart from feeling, like a temporary unconsciousness. Quietly asking them not to talk about him, I walk away to wash any part of him off me. I will not say his name; my brain blocks my lips from making the sound. He has moved on and away, leaving me behind. My memory of our love is now in a deep, visionless vault of memories. Scars so deep, I see them every day when I look in the mirror, secluded in my private hell of secrets with the Sister.

ॐ ॐ ॐ

Senior year blows by like a thunderstorm in Kansas. It comes, does what it came to do, and leaves. My debris spreads behind me, and I wonder if there's anything left to collect. I trudge through it with my shrapnel-filled heart. Can I salvage my dignity? The demons follow me, my memories of Adam like a ghost floating through the school hallways. My friends anchor me the best they can and include me in their social lives. Disengaging from deep or meaningful conversation, I look to alcohol, my trusted friend, to keep me present among the living, tolerating relationships with the opposite sex but sabotaging them from ever maturing into anything material or memorable. I break some hearts while I tow them behind me, unwilling to be loved, dragging my sinful, heavy baggage everywhere I go, not willing to add anything else to the load I carry.

One breath, one blink, one step forward to pass the days is my goal. I've never gone back to church and see no reason to. I set my sights ahead to college, trying to muster up the old Jules. The Jules with dreams of a future, with laughter in her step. Next goal: get the hell out of here.

CHAPTER ELEVEN

Sister, pack your rosary. College moving day is here. I pray new faces and the opportunity to fulfill my dreams will somehow manage to fill my memory bank with happier stories. The patch of glue that has kept me together all summer must help me make it through college life. The dream of helping other teen girls motivates me, and I declare my major in social work. Giving others hope and reasons to survive might help me move forward, too.

The family van is parked in the garage, the engine running. I sit silently on the bench seat in the back, surrounded by comforting new college ensembles.

"I wanted to check the map one more time," Dad says before hopping in the driver's seat.

Mom buckles herself into the passenger seat. "I made sandwiches."

"It's an hour drive, Mom. Okay, give me mine. It's just like our summer vacation road trips. We usually ate our sandwiches before we even got down the driveway." All of us laugh.

"I'll take mine, too. Why not—for old times' sake," Dad says.

Watching the familiar sights and sounds disappear behind me, each bite of my sandwich brings some comfort to allay my fears. My chest aches with doubt. Can I start a new life alone?

Sliding the door of the van open, I jump out and land on both feet of my new turf. The Prentice Hall sign at the concrete entrance tells me I'm where I'm supposed to be.

"You did good, Dad. This is it."

I smile at the thought of what I just did, figuratively and literally. Taking a step and then another, I walk straight for the front door of the dorm, briefly note my reflection, and like what I see. As I peer inside at the growing group of residents, girls and more girls mingle around. Lines form, and suitcases and boxes are pushed, rolled, dragged in every direction. Following the alphabetized signs, I look for "K" — Kane — and step up to a smiling face.

"Juliette." The name Elizabeth flashes in my head as Kane flows from my mouth. "Juliette Kane."

"Welcome to Prentice Hall. Your room is on the second floor." Keys are dangled before me, and I swoop them up.

"Please initial here for the keys, take a welcome packet, and see you tomorrow at our information meeting."

Initialing JK on the line, I turn to scan the reception area. Mom and Dad enter, burdened with boxes and baskets and toting a suitcase behind them. I sprint to relieve them of the excess weight, and we shuffle toward the elevator.

"My room's on the second floor. Push number two," I say, grabbing stuff from underneath Mom's arms. We shuffle out of the elevator and down the carpeted hallway to Room 213.

I slide the key into the keyhole and slowly open the door to the unknown. Leaning in, I speak through the crack, "Hello, anyone here?"

Silence answers me. I push open the door to find sterile white walls that scale up to the twelve-foot ceilings. Two extra-long twin beds are pushed against the walls, built-in dresser drawers accompanied by two sliding closet doors, and two desks randomly placed in the middle of the room.

"Mom, Dad, you can drop those bags in the corner by the window. I wonder which bed is mine," I say, rifling through the paperwork they gave me.

"Okay, we are going to make another trip down to the van," Dad says, turning toward the door.

I can hear Mom talking to everyone she encounters in the hallway.

"Hello. How are you? What room are you in? My daughter Jules is in 213."

Rolling my eyes, I shake my head and glance in the large mirror nestled between the closet doors. Throwing my hands up and reaching for the sky, I feel light, my limbs weightless, my feet are dancing to the to the music in my head, a smile spreads across my face.

Dad comes back in, pushes open the door, and Mom is two steps behind him, arms filled with clothes on hangers, her eyes peering over the pile.

"One more trip should do it," Dad says, dropping his cargo on the bed I declared mine.

Together we walk down to the elevator, sadness growing in Mom's eyes.

"Thanks for all your help," I say, wrapping my arms around her.

"Study hard and stay out of trouble," she says. Her words practically drain the blood from my veins; fatigue flows in and weakens my legs with each step.

Dad hangs his arm over my shoulder, and we walk to the van. Words don't need to fill the silence.

"Bye, Dad." Stepping back up onto the sidewalk, I stand in front of the van. I mouth, "I love you." I turn and walk down the sidewalk to the dorm.

Sitting on the floor, I unpack, my skeleton life spread all around me. The door pops open, and in bounces a ball of positive wildfire energy.

"Hello." I stand.

"Hi, it's Kim. I'm your roommate."

"Hello, Kim. I picked this bed if that's okay. I really don't care which one is mine."

"Sure, that's okay. This is my mom and dad."

"Nice to meet you. You just missed my parents by a few minutes. Do you need help bringing stuff up?"

"No, that's what little sisters are for," Kim says, a big smile on her face.

Kim is a tall beautiful blonde with waves of sunshiny hair falling across her shoulders, eyes of blue, oldest girl of five from a town forty-five minutes away from Kent. The rhapsody of her enthusiasm to be at college radiates from her pores. *Sister, does she have a story, too?*

Kim hugs her family while escorting them down the hallway and sends them on their way home. She enters the room with the last of her treasures. "I brought some beer, want one?" she says.

"We are going to get along just fine, Kim." I smile and reach my hand out.

Popping the cap off, I walk over to the window. Darkness fills the sky, day one of college coming to an end as I turn back to finish emptying the last box.

Plopping our exhausted bodies on the floor, we raise our Little Kings beer and toast. "Here's to a new start. I sure could use one," I say.

"Right back at ya," Kim says, giggling between sips of beer.

"We'd better get some sleep. Orientation starts in a few hours."

🐌 🐌 🐌

The alarm clock blares in my ear, and the smell of the stale beer on my nightstand turns my stomach. The chattering voices and movement outside our dorm room door pique my interest.

I crack open the door in search of free coffee. The freshman populous is in high gear, weaving past strangers on their search for the shared bathroom and shower stalls at the end of the hall.

Kim and I hustle to get ready for freshman orientation; dancing around each other, we feel the awkwardness of new roommates cohabiting in close quarters. We check our campus map and throw on our backpacks. Slamming the door behind us, nothing but fear stands in our way.

We sit among the hundreds of new freshmen in the large auditorium, half listening, half searching the new faces, studying them for clues of their past. Who here has secrets they are hiding?

Meeting new people is difficult for me; I prepare my answers ahead of time, never wanting to be caught off guard. "Where are you from?" is followed by family, friends, and boyfriend questions. At first, I come off as rude, with short answers or no answers at all, as if I did not hear the question. I have mastered the question-and-answer period of new conversations, but I don't want to talk about my past. I am here to talk about my future because it must be better than my past. No, I tell myself, it *will* be better.

CHAPTER TWELVE

Spring is here and the flower buds burst forth from the frosted dirt. We survived the first semester, and it flows right into the next. Mornings are crisp with frost-covered green grass. Later, the afternoon sun fills the big blue sky. School is a routine, something I enjoy and count on. Winding down from the day, finding comfort in my room, and reading my new syllabus with professor guidelines and rules, I arrange my new textbooks on my desk. I kick back, entranced by the brilliant sun slowly dropping through the clouds and filtering through the treetops. Another day is ending. Resting my head on the back of my chair, I slowly close my eyes. I enjoy the last of the day's warm sunlight on my face and the peaceful quiet of the dorm. Abruptly, I jump up. I am standing. Blasting, blaring horns fill the room, and garbled loud voices boom through the intercom. It's the fire alarm. I wait for instructions in hopes it will be a false alarm, but they are quickly quashed when someone announces, "This is not a drill, ladies. Calmly move to the stairways and exit the building."

Glancing down at my attire, I shake my head in disgust at my mismatched socks, ripping them off and throwing them on the floor. Jumping up, I scour my closet for a sweatshirt, something to cover my Rolling Stones T-shirt with its giant red tongue. I grab a baseball hat to finish off my sweatpants ensemble, tuck the uncombed flyways underneath it, and slip my toes into my flip-flops. It is going to be chilly outside, so I zip up my sweatshirt to the neckline.

"Oh my God, Kim, why do you always look good? Look at me." She raises her eyebrows.

"Let's go. Your ridiculous outfit won't mean a thing if there is a real fire."

"My luck, the firemen will be drop-dead gorgeous, and they'll be fighting to resuscitate you," I say. "Me . . . not so much." Laughing in unison, we exit.

"We don't want those designer jeans catching on fire," she says as she puts on her jean jacket. Damn her, she looks cute.

The hallway is packed with evacuees, disgruntled estrogen trailing toward the stairs. Waiting for a break in the flow, Kim and I cut into the crowd and head in the direction of the exit sign. Two by two, we walk down the brightly illuminated stairwells, the emergency lights blinding me and spotlighting my outfit. As we exit through the double metal doors on the bottom floor, the stinging, cold air outside hits my face.

"This way, girls." A college staffer ushers us away from the building toward the empty parking lot. We stop at the edge of the grass and watch as the crowd grows.

I stomp my feet side to side, one by one, to keep the circulation moving, and a chill moves up from my toes — chicken skin covers my body. I look up at the clear black sky. The sun is gone, and I search briefly for my stars of the past, next to the clear white moon.

Bursts of laughter erupt; the girls see the mass of testosterone headed in our direction. The girls hoot and holler, the sound echoing between the concrete dorms. The all-male dorm from across the street marches toward us. The bright lights from the parking lot shine down on the male regatta.

I see an outline of a person approaching at a fast pace, shadows of light playing tricks on my vision. My mind puts the pieces of this puzzle together, trying to make sense of the flying fabric flapping in the wind behind this solo silhouette shadow coming my way. It's like a cartoon scene, and someone resembling a superhero suddenly appears out of a cloud of smoke. A mystery nothing becomes something when a body shadow forms. What is it? Blowing in the wind, a knee-length, loose garment streams behind this shadow that gallops in my direction.

Humming to distract myself from the cold air, I wiggle my freezing toes in my summer flip-flops. Counting always calms my nerves . . . one, two, three, four, five, six. Slowly I lift my head to get a glimpse, but I peek two counts too early. He takes one more giant step and stops. Standing in front of me is a blond, blue-eyed male in a blue bathrobe. Untied, the bathrobe hangs open. His hands stuffed inside the pockets, he postures himself in front of me as though we're at a standoff.

I stare at his beach-body chest. What is this guy, a lifeguard? Tan, abs, biceps — he would be a ten if he were a few inches taller. I work my way back up to his ashen lips; chilled soft pink cheeks cover his face, and his cobalt-blue eyes meet mine. At that instant, he says, "Hi, my name is Levi, and you have the most beautiful blue eyes I have ever seen."

The terry cloth bathrobe has stopped in front of me. Rolling my eyes, I think, why me?

Panicked, I'm jarred by my heart pulsating like a jackhammer in my chest. *Boom, boom, boom.* I can hear it. Can he? He is talking, and I struggle to hear his words. He says, "I have seen you around campus."

I'm shocked by his words. You have seen me? I have never seen you before, is what I am thinking. My mind tries to pull up some memory of our paths crossing while he keeps talking, and still reeling at his first words, I miss it all.

I shake my head to stop my humming. I swallow to clear my ears, my own heart beating so loud, it's all I can hear; it's blocking his words.

He continues talking and says, "I thought, why not take this opportunity to introduce myself. I saw you standing over here, so here I am." He spreads his arms open wide. "Who can resist a man in a blue bathrobe?"

I smile at the sound of the word "bathrobe." Laughing out loud from deep in my gut, I say, "Nice to meet you, Levi."

"And your name is?"

"Jules," I respond, crisp and sharp. "Levi, I am impressed with the boldness of the bathrobe, but I would keep moving on. You do look cold."

He shifts right to left and places his hands back in his pockets. He tugs the fabric to cover his bare chest.

I am saved by the bell; blaring horns are followed by broken tones of the megaphone. "All clear. You can all return to your dorms."

Our eyes meet for one long second, and I turn to walk toward my dorm. I look back over my shoulder for Kim, who luckily isn't too far away. She hurriedly navigates through the crowd to join me. Irritated, my eyes bulge. I roll them in Levi's direction. She knows I am trying to tell her something, and she leans in close to me. "Get me the hell out of here," I say. "Save me from that guy."

She gently turns and asks, "Which guy, that blond one? What in the world is he wearing?

"A robe — a blue bathrobe!"

"Hmm, interesting," Kim says.

Grabbing her by the hand, I pull her close, and we walk arm in arm toward the front entrance of the dorm. "Definitely not the hot fireman, but he was hot," I say. "I sure do attract the good ones, don't I?" We giggle together.

I turn back one last time to look over my shoulder at this guy named Levi. He hasn't moved. He watches my body move away from his. I flash him half a smile for effort. Good move, Blue Robe. I turn and keep walking away. You must have me mistaken for someone else, I think. We have never seen each other before.

This stranger in a bathrobe has rustled my conscience. I toss and turn in my restless sleep, and his words have me dreaming deep. Jumping from cloud to cloud, I see faces popping in and out. I ask each one, "Have I seen you before? Did I look at you? Talk to you?"

I wake with questions about my existence. The faces I saw in my dreams, do I know them? He said he saw me on campus. Did I see him but not really *see* him? What else is right in front of me? Faces I am not seeing, songs I am not hearing? Am I living life or just living?

§ § §

Is this guy following me? This Levi guy is everywhere. He said he saw me on campus. How is it that I didn't see him? Too caught up in the baggage I keep toting around?

"Good morning, Jules. Have a nice day," a yell comes from across the street.

"Morning," I say, raising my head to see who it is. Levi?

Later, as I eat my lunch in the cafeteria, I hear that voice again. "Enjoy your lunch, Jules."

Choking on a bite of my second piece of pizza, I sputter, "Yes, thanks." I quickly put my pizza down with visions of me with a double chin, the freshman fifteen whispering in my ear.

Walking into the gym, there he is waving across the basketball court to me. Was he always there? Was I blindfolded to the living souls around me? Did my trampled heart never let my bruised eyes see him?

As I walk back to my dorm, I see faces of strangers who might not be strangers after all. Have I passed them every day, same time, same place, and am only now seeing them for the first time?

My hands quiver. I sweep the bottom of my backpack and dig in the crevasses for my dorm key, my existence shaken. I am existing, not embracing the joys of life or appreciating the people around me. *Sister, I miss my old self.* The fighter, the thrill seeker who does what she wants, when she wants. The joy that makes me smile is missing. I need to get it back.

Whirling from today's discoveries, I stand patiently waiting for the elevator door to open. There's a commotion back at the entrance lobby — the high-pitched screech of a chair moving across the tile floor followed by a loud voice calling my name.

"Jules . . . Juliette, are you still there? Jules, come back, you have a delivery."

What, me? I turn my head to make sure I've heard correctly. Our eyes meet. Her head bobs up and down, and she points off to the left.

"Are you sure they are for me? Jules Kane?"

"Yes, that is the name on the envelope. They were delivered about an hour ago."

I am blinded by the brilliant flower arrangement; the vibrant red rose petals prance tall on top of pine-green stems. Looking closer, I notice the killer thorns hiding under soft petal leaves. I move closer, counting the bundled blossoms, one, two, three, four, and I see it, deeply tucked between the silky soft petals and thorns: a white envelope. Confused, I look back at her.

She repeats, "They have your name on it, Jules. I swear."

I smile, my heart beating faster, and it's as though a valve has opened to let love flow back in. Unlocking the vault of the past, I see his face, hear his infectious laugh that makes my cheeks hurt while my smile gets bigger.

"They must be from him," I whisper. "Maybe he is here?"

Sister, are you answering the sinner's prayers?

"Open the card. Who sent you those lovely roses?" she says, leaning over her desk.

Slowly inching closer, I drag my feet up to the counter as if I'm moving through quicksand. I lean in to inhale the bouquet of love — the springtime sweetness fills the air.

Focusing on the envelope that will solve the mystery, I stretch my hand out to reach for it, avoiding the prickly thorns. My hand quivers as I place it in my palm. I fixate on the writing of my name. J-U-L-E-S. Slowly I turn the sealed envelope over, slip my fingers into the crease, and lift the edge, cracking open the seal. For a second, I pause and postpone pulling out the card, staring at the blank backside, my heart opening, dancing with the hope of love, fluttering with euphoria. Deep breaths in through my nose, holding it in, lungs full of blossoming courage.

Swiftly I turn it over and read the words out loud. "Will you go out with me tonight? Blue Robe–Levi."

What the fuck! Cursing the gods, I crush the written note in my palm, choking the words from my existence, emptying my lungs of cold, stale air.

One step forward, two steps back. I drop my head in disappointment and shake my head. Now what the hell do I do? Why is this guy bothering me? Doesn't he know I am trying to get happy?

Clutching it like a football, I stuff the vase under my arm as I storm to the elevator. I charge down the hallway, kicking open the door to my dorm room. Startled, Kim pushes away from her desk as she tries to see who is behind this massive burst of roses.

I yell, "He sent me fucking flowers!"

"Who sent you flowers?" says Kim.

"The guy from the parking lot — the one in the blue robe."

"Why are you so mad that he sent you flowers?" Kim asks.

Answers swirl in my head. I stand in silence looking at her before I say, "Because I don't want flowers from this guy Levi."

I hand her the card, and she reads it, then raises her eyes to look back at me. "Just go out to dinner with him. What are you afraid of?"

"What am I afraid of?" I whisper under my breath. *Sister, I'm afraid of everything.*

I turn and throw my broken heart onto the bed.

CHAPTER THIRTEEN

Slouched comfortably in my black desk chair, I prop a schoolbook open on my lap and stretch my legs out, resting my feet comfortably on top of my desk. My eye catches the efflorescence of soft flower petals. Every rose is perfectly wrapped, layer over layer, like a baby wrapped in a blanket. I start to count: one, two, three, four, five, six, seven, eight, nine, ten, and eleven. Eleven seems odd. Where is the twelfth? Eleven red roses sprawled in an hourglass vase at the edge of my desk. Papers strewn across my desk cover half of the vase as they lie in no order, but all are related to political science. I stand to reach over the top of my desk to organize my paper pile. My face crosses the path of brilliant roses, and I breathe in a fresh, clean smell: sweet floral bitterness.

I close my eyes and see him handing me my corsage. The corsage I wore to my high school junior dance — three red roses, baby's breath, a crisp white ribbon draped all around them in a beautiful bundle. I glance down and see it on my wrist, my long red satin dress sweeping the floor, his black tux with a red bow tie and cummerbund. Matching like bookends, we were a couple, we were together, we were happy. Glancing back at the vase of eleven roses, I'm disgusted with myself for thinking they were from him. Does he ever think of me the way I continue to think of him?

I slowly slip into a sulking trance of the past when I am startled by a jolting, ringing noise. It's my dorm room phone. Ring, ring, oh my God . . . quiet, please. Ringing. I contemplate not answering it. I anticipate it is Kim trying to get ahold of me, same old speech. "You need to go out. It's good for you. Have some fun with us." I have heard it all before.

I stand closer, stalking the phone, counting the rings, hoping after each one that it will be the last. Ring, ring, ring. It's not stopping, and I can't take it anymore. I swipe the phone off the wall to choke out the badgering sound. I bring it close to my ear.

Anticipating Kim's convincing voice, I am taken aback by something else. Not a hello or gentle greeting. Instead I hear a deep voice. "Hey, we have a dinner date. You ready?"

I pull the phone away from my ear and look at the receiver. It's him — the guy who was standing outside in his blue robe during the fire drill. Holy shit, it sounds like him. It *must* be him. He is waiting for me to reply. Thoughts are running through my head. Perhaps if I don't reply, he'll get the message. The answer is no!

He speaks again. "I know you're still there. This is Levi. Are you ready?"

My mind races, searching for an excuse.

He says, "You have five minutes to be in the lobby, or I'm coming up to drag you out of your room. We're going out to dinner. See you in the lobby in five minutes, got it?"

My head swirls in blank space. No excuse yet. I look up at the calendar on the wall above the phone. Month, March. Date, tenth, blank, nothing written in, nothing in pen, nothing in pencil. Nothing planned but I have an excuse; I just can't seem to get it out. I'm sick, say that. My conscience talks back. That's a lie. You don't lie. Moments pass. I press the receiver back to my ear only to hear the buzz of a dial tone filling the silence. I slam the phone into its cradle.

"Damn you, Blue Robe, you hung up on me." Damn you, Jules, you need to start learning to lie.

Abruptly changing course, my heart races at the thought of him coming up here and seeing me like this. I turn to look in the mirror. What a mess! Flushed ruby-red cheeks, hair swirling in every direction. Reasoning with my temper, whispering under my breath, I ask myself, what do I do with this guy? I didn't ask him to call! Why doesn't he just leave me alone? The arrogant tone of his voice, persistent and demanding. How dare you talk to me like that! Blue Robe Guy, you bug the shit out of me. I need to deal with him now. He might follow through on his threat and come up here, unescorted. That's all I need — a scene on my dorm floor. I will go downstairs and extinguish him and fill his mind with noes: no, no, and no, and the fire will be out.

Rummaging through the bottom drawer, I look for a pair of jeans that will comfort me. Am I nervous or is it anger? I grab a pink V-neck T-shirt off the hanger and throw it over my head. I grab my bathroom bucket filled with my makeup and toothbrush and sprint down the hall to the communal bathroom. When I open my makeup bag, I contemplate where I should start. Sifting through it, I grab the blush and brush some color over my cheeks, sweep soft pink gloss across my lips.

Sprinting back to my room, I throw my bucket of toiletries on my unmade bed and slip on a pair of black flip-flops. I reach for my room key, glance back at my purse, and leave it in place. I am making a quick trip downstairs. I will be back in five minutes. I walk out of my dorm room, slamming the door behind me — it locks automatically. My anger builds more and more with each step I take toward the elevator doors. Down the hall, I pass open doors but don't look in to say hello. Just keep walking, I tell myself, taking large steps on the triangle-patterned carpet.

I face the elevator, blinking uncontrollably at the shiny silver door. Repeatedly my finger firmly pushes the round down button. It lights up, but I continue to press the button anyway. The elevator door opens. I take two steps in and swing around to stand in the middle of the elevator. Push L for lobby.

Under the bright elevator spotlight, I start rehearsing what I'm going to say. I am on stage, ready with my lines. You . . . Levi guy. You, or anyone else, do not tell me what to do and don't ever hang up on me. Do not call or send flowers. With a smile on my face, I lick my slippery lips, confidence coming from perfect lip gloss. I'm planning a short exchange. In no time, I will be back in my sweatpants, hair up in a high ponytail, swiveling in my black desk chair, my feet resting on my desk.

The door cracks open, and I take my first step forward. Abruptly, I stop. What the . . . ? Eye to eye, only inches apart, Blue Robe Guy blocks my way. Shocked by his closeness, I take one giant step back into the elevator. His big smile, wavy short blond hair combed back, light-blue short-sleeve polo shirt with collar up, biceps bulging from the elastic ribbing, form-fitting Levi blue jeans with beige Dockside shoes are blocking me from my exit. A red rose in one hand, his other hand, open and welcoming, reaches inside the elevator, inviting me to embrace it. My anger dissolves, and his gorgeous blue eyes beckon me. I'm speechless because my speech seems useless. My eyes reexamine his bulging biceps; I follow his tan arm that is reaching out to me. I see his hand and know what he wants, but I'm unable to move. The door starts to close; he reaches in for me.

Gently he guides me out of the elevator. "I have an exciting evening planned for us," he says. "This is the last rose to make it a full dozen." Opening my fingers, he places the green stem in my grip. "I'm glad you could make it." With a devious smirk on his face, he turns with me in tow. I don't resist and follow right behind him as he effortlessly guides me out of the lobby, out the front door, down the sidewalk to his car. He pauses for a second before he opens the passenger side door for me. I get in, and he gently closes the door after I settle in. What is wrong with me, getting into a stranger's car? Or is he really a stranger?

❧ ❧ ❧

The blue Volkswagen purrs up the hill to the dorm. Vibrating music escapes through the sunroof as it screeches to a halt. The dorm building is perched in front of us, brightly lit by security lights. It's 3:00 a.m., and darkness surrounds the wee hour as the date comes to an end. Nervously, I tap my fingers on the cold metal window handle, feverishly rolling it down while his body leans closer into my space.

His fingertips weave between mine. "You look nervous," he says. "I'm not a serial killer." My cheeks rise in a shy smile. "Thank you for going out with me. I had a wonderful night."

"Well, that's good, Levi. You didn't give me much of a choice. You could be the Blue Robe Stalker."

He says, "Will you go out with the BRS tomorrow night?"

I smile, hanging my head low as rumbled confusion runs through my head. How do you end a date?

Freeing my hand from his, I reach for the door handle, open the door, and close it behind me. I turn back, lean inside the window, and say, "Thank you for dinner, Levi — the Levi who wears Levi's." I turn and hurriedly slip away into my dorm's brightly lit entrance.

Quietly ,I enter my room, the heavy door groaning at its hinges. Kim stirs in her bed. Blinded by the darkness, I tiptoe from memory across the floor to my bed. Dropping my keys and my shirt along the way, I let out a sigh of relief. My fingertips find my satin-covered bed, and I pull back the covers and sink my butt onto the mattress. I kick off my flip-flops, wiggle out of my jeans. BOOM! The lights go on, and I try to adjust to the unexpected illumination.

Kim sits straight up in bed with an enormous smile on her face. "I'm guessing you had a good time, Jules, with the blue robe. I was worried about you. He could be a serial killer."

"That's funny, that's exactly what he said."

"What time is it?"

"Three o'clock in the morning," I whisper.

She giggles, throwing her blonde hair back on her pillow, killing the light.

Pulling the covers over my face to hide my contagious smile, I pinch myself. This really is happening.

𝄞 𝄞 𝄞

Morning sunrays pierce through the blinds. Friday night's date replays in my brain, and I don't want to leave my bed's warm cocoon. I sluggishly dress for my Saturday morning racquetball game, already late. Moving slower than usual, I shove my racquet and can of new balls into my backpack, throw it over my shoulder, and take the stairs to the lobby. After checking my watch one more time, I push the front doors open and start my jog to the gym.

"Good morning, Juliette," Levi yells from across the street. "We have another date tonight at seven."

Stopping in my tracks, I narrow my gaze. "First of all, only two people call me Juliette, my mom and Sister Elizabeth, and you are neither of those. And I never said yes."

"I decided for you, Jules." He grins, leaning against his car, arms folded. "We're going bowling. Be ready this time — not like last night."

Hands on my hips, I walk closer to him. "Don't you sleep? Have you been waiting here all night for me to pass by?"

His eyes twinkle. "I would wait all night for you, Jules."

Breathless, I realize he is tugging on my baggage, slowly throwing things out, lightening my heavy load. If only . . . I stop myself.

Drawing in a breath, I exhale slowly, grounding myself. "See you tonight, Levi. Date number two with the serial killer."

CHAPTER FOURTEEN

owling, really? Who the heck takes a girl bowling? A geek. Is this guy a geek? Does he have his
own ball and shoes? Now that scares me even more
than a second date. Who is this guy? I glance at the
clock: 6:10 p.m. I am getting ready for the date that
I don't want to go on, or so I say to myself. I have a
distraction; I'm making a baby step forward. Nervous, I giggle while putting on my makeup. Without
feeling guilty, I try to smile. I have something to look
forward to.

The moment Kim walks into the dorm room, I give
her the news. "Get ready. We're going bowling."

She crosses her eyes in confusion. "What? What
do you mean, we are going bowling?"

"Yes," I say with a smirk. "You heard correctly.
Bowling. I'm going and you're going with me." I tap
my foot impatiently. "Just get dressed, okay? I don't
want to go on this date alone, but I have a sudden
urge to go bowling."

Levi picks us up promptly at 7:00 and only seems a
little surprised at Kim's presence. We are soon at the
alley, and once we've gotten our shoes and a lane, I'm
surprised at my reaction. Who would have thought

bowling could be so liberating? And yet here I am at the alley, feeling a lightness I haven't in over a year.

Outright laughter escapes my lips, and I'm hunched over, letting loose giggles from deep in my soul. The ball leaves my three fingers. It barrels down the striped wood bowling lane, crashing into pins, breaking my life wide open.

"Strike!" Strutting, I return to my seat.

"Anyone want a beer?" Kim says, walking toward the bar.

"That's not going to help your bowling, just saying."

"Is that a yes, Jules? Levi?"

"Yes."

"Yes."

Levi plops down next to me. "Having fun yet?"

"Since I haven't bowled in a while, I am glad I'm not a total embarrassment."

"Embarrassment? I need to step up my game," he says.

Kim returns from the bar and hands us both beers.

"Good timing. You're up, Kim." Levi points toward the lane.

Putting her beer down and picking up her ball, she says, "You two are in trouble now."

Competition explodes between us and competitive plays of strategy emerge. Frame after frame, we bowl for hours amid whoops and hollers of fun. I laugh — an unforced laugh, a happy laugh that has not come out in a long time. It flows from my body with an urgency to escape.

"Kim cracks me up. Jules, did you know her before college?"

"No, but I sure got lucky when I ended up with her as a roommate, didn't I, Levi?"

"Yes, you did. I'll have to fix her up," he responds when Kim is within hearing distance.

Kim eyes me from behind Levi's back, shaking her head no.

"I'll just hang out with you two. Thanks anyways, Levi."

Still a perfect gentleman, Levi doesn't argue, although I wonder what he thinks about having a chaperone. We wrap up our last game and head to the dorm.

CHAPTER FIFTEEN

"Yes, he does have his own bowling ball and shoes." I shake my head at the thought as I talk on the phone with my high school girlfriend Nancy.

"I haven't heard from you in a while, Jules. That means you're dating someone, aren't you?"

"We go out. I wouldn't say it's dating, but it's been going on since March."

"I knew it!" she says with a laugh. "So who is he?"

"His name is Levi. You should come for the weekend sometime and meet him before summer break."

"Not sure I can get away, but I'll let you know," she says. "So how are your classes?"

"School's good—only a few more weekends before I'll be home for the summer. Put the word out for me. I need a summer job."

"For sure," she answers. "I've heard of a few part-time secretary jobs."

"Get me in! I need some money for school next year."

"Will do. Miss going out and partying with you." Her voice is wistful.

"Ya, me too. Wish I could remember senior year. Oh, well," I say. "Keep in touch, Nancy. Thanks for calling."

Since March, we have spent a lot of time at the bowling alley. Turns out Levi works there, studies there, and sometimes sleeps there. Essentially, he works every free moment he can between his classes at school, desperately needing the money to help pay for housing expenses and books. I never really ask about it, but I know it weighs on him.

"I'm buying you a bowling ball for your birthday."

"That sounds like a threat. Throw in shoes, and we're committed." I laugh with a tinge of dread and fear at the words that come from my lips. "Get back to studying," I say, trying to change the subject. "Let's get something to eat in a bit before you go to work."

"And by the way," I continue, "you don't have to buy me a birthday present. Save your money for school."

Whispering in my ear, Levi says, "I love you. You make my life better."

Cringing at the words any normal person would love to hear, I take my time responding. "Thank you. I am not brave enough to love again. I fell in love, once."

"You will, Jules. You will love me."

"Study! Freshman year of college is over in four days."

"I have something that's on my mind. It's kinda important."

"Study, Levi. Enough talking."

Looking around my dorm room, it feels cold and empty without all the pictures Kim and I hung up during our year together. The school year had some sweet surprises, Levi for one. He has brought positive energy back into my life. Next year brings so many opportunities, and the prospect of volunteering with a teen group excites me, but it's bittersweet that this school year is ending. Packing my clothes and emptying my dorm room between finals, I've watched the boxes pile high, waiting to be sealed.

"I talked to my friend Nancy today. She happened to call my dorm room when I was studying. She thinks she has a summer job for me already."

"Wow, awesome," Levi says.

Noting some distress in the way his head hangs low, I take in the rest of him. His body looks exhausted and beat. I write it off to the stress of finals, packing, and next year's living arrangements. Smiling to myself, I wonder if he wants to talk about living together next year.

"I'm going to head back to my dorm. I have some packing to do myself. I hope all your stuff fits in my bug, Jules." Levi stares at my clothes and boxes on his way out.

"It will. See you tomorrow. I'll be ready around seven o'clock."

First year of college is over. All my paperwork is done, everything is signed, keys have been turned in. I am in my room finishing the last of my packing.

Kim has already left. We said our goodbyes, laughed, and cried, even though I will see her next week. Stowing the last pair of shoes in my suitcase, I straddle the bag. My body weight crashes down on it, suffocating its contents, and I zip it closed. My phone is ringing. I look up at the clock and it's 7:05 p.m. I don't answer; I know it's Levi. He must be ready to go. Grabbing the last of my luggage, I hurry out the door, stumble down the hallway with overflowing last-minute items under my arms, and trudge to the elevator for the last time as a freshman.

The elevator door opens at the lobby level, revealing Levi, who is standing there with clenched jaw, tension in his face. Avoiding eye contact, he reaches into the elevator and grabs my bulging suitcase and carries it out to the car. Is he mad at me? Did I do something? He didn't greet me with the oh-so-familiar smile and tenderhearted touch of his lips on my cheek.

Polluting the silence, I walk swiftly to catch up to him. "Levi," I yell out.

"Keep walking, Jules."

"Hello. Did something happen?" Swiftly I walk up to where he stands at the open trunk.

"We will talk in the car," he says, running his hand through his hair.

"Are you mad at me?"

"I'm starting to get a little irritated." He crosses his arms over his chest. "Start putting your stuff in the backseat."

He walks around to the passenger door, opens it, and waits for me to toss my duffle bag onto the backseat. I juggle my purse and other bags, dropping them on the front seat floor, and slide into the blue Beetle. He slams the door closed behind me.

The Beetle backs out, roars away from Prentice Hall. I roll the window down, my hair blowing in the wind, throw my hand out, look back, and wave goodbye.

"See you in September."

Levi remains focused on the road ahead.

"My mom wants to know if you are staying for dinner," I say.

"It will be late. I should head home."

"You can stay and head home tomorrow. I'll deal with my mom."

"I would never do that to you. I know you aren't looking forward to moving home for the summer."

"Okay."

Levi turns up the radio, and I take that as a sign he isn't ready to talk. I adjust to the silence, soaking in the rolling hills and watching the tall oak trees whisk by my side of the car window. Semitrucks barrel past on the other side.

The Beetle makes its way to Hardy Road and rolls up the driveway to my house. He pulls up on the hand break and turns the car off. Not pausing, he jumps out, walks around the car, and opens my door.

"It was nice chatting with you!" I say, rolling my eyes, biting my cheek before I say more.

I swing my legs around and climb out, maneuvering myself over the bags at my feet. I stand brushing my body against him, hoping to change his mood. He reaches out to grab me with urgency, and I feel the pressure of his strong hands; the rage inside him gets my attention.

"What is going on?" I ask.

With his fingers locked behind my back, he looks down at me and says, "I met with my counselors. I'm leaving school. I cannot go back."

My knees weaken and buckle like broken twigs.

"When did you think you would tell me?"

Panic sets in. Oh no. I knew I shouldn't have answered that phone call that Friday night. *Oh, Sister, I fell for the fucking rose.*

His warm breath is heavy on my face, his neck veins bulging, the grip so tight around my waist, I'm not sure which one of us is more afraid.

"I leave in two days for the Air Force basic training boot camp in Texas. I cannot pay for school next year. I need to help my mom support my sister and brothers. I am on my own, Jules. You don't know what that is like." His voice cracks, and he pushes me an arm's length away and closes his eyes, visibly shaken. The stress shows in his creased brow.

"I didn't tell you sooner because I wanted you to enjoy your last few days of school." He stares at the ground but keeps going. "I want your memories to be positive, happy ones. I didn't want to cause you to worry. You were happy, and I like seeing you happy. I waited to tell you, and I'm sorry."

My voice is shallow as I say, "I let you . . . I let you into my life. I gave you what I could. I guess it wasn't enough, and now you're leaving me."

A bomb detonates inside my body, and the memories, still so raw, resurface. I have felt this before: the fear, the resentment, the anger, the panic of someone leaving me, and being abandoned.

I yell, "You are leaving me in two days!"

I roll my tongue back and forth across my quivering lips. Mouth dry, I swallow.

"Go! Leave, Levi. Walk away. I know how this story ends." My neck tightens as the blood flows to my temples. I bob my head up and down, loosening the tension.

And as though I'm confirming it for myself, I realize my life is taking an unexpected turn, and this chapter is about to end. Grabbing tight onto the front of his shirt, I cinch his T-shirt between my fingers, digging my fingertips into his chest bones, trying to scratch away his words. Tension drains out of my hands, releasing all the pain from my broken heart. My fingers go limp. What am I fighting for? He wants to leave? Leave!

Stepping back, stepping away from the hurt, I let my hands fall free from his shirt, withdrawing from him one giant step backward at a time. I tug down on my shirt, wrenching his words from my heart.

I turn and my feet hit the hard concrete path to the house as I dart away from him.

"My God, will you just listen?" His voice sounds louder behind me.

Quick to follow, Levi grabs me with both hands, his arms wrapped tight from behind, his strong arms binding me. I come to a standstill and collapse forward, hinged at the waist, swinging like a broken doll. My hair sweeps the ground.

Lifting me back up, he presses his warm body against mine and cradles me for a moment. "Stop, Jules. Listen to me, look at me!" Spinning me around, he frames my face with his hands, forcing my head back up. I gaze deep into his blue eyes, the same ones that captured my attention the day I met him.

"I am not leaving you behind," he says. "I do not want to live another day without you. I love you. I fall more in love with you every day. You are all I need."

I say nothing and stand numb. Silence is a killer.

He drops his arms and slowly backs away from me. "Say something, Jules," he yells. "Say anything!"

I hear him fiddling with his keys, waiting for my words. He opens the trunk, grabs my suitcase, placing it on the driveway.

Again, he says, "Jules."

Frozen, I stand watching him walk around to the driver's side door. He opens it, looks at me one more time over the VW roof, and gets back into the bug.

I stand swollen with pain. I do nothing, say nothing, and watch the Beetle pull out of the driveway.

The second it starts to roll away, away from me, my heart begins to pound heavily as I try to pretend everything is all right. But my feet are telling my head something else, and frantically, I start chasing after something I didn't think I needed: love. I left part of my heart in that car. Arms waving, I run as fast as I can after him. He never looks back, or does he? Never sees me chasing after him, or maybe he does, but I keep running anyway until the top of the Volkswagen disappears into the setting sun.

CHAPTER SIXTEEN

Levi is gone. I let him go. I didn't have the courage to keep him, my mind still silencing my voice. I didn't have the courage to leave, so he left without me. He rolled right out of my life, and I watched him do it. My heart hurts just the same.

Being home is hard. I have many trepidations about being in this house for the summer, especially without Levi around. My house — treasured by my inner child, hated by my taken child. As much as I do not want to be here, I am here. My mom, my love for her as her child, wars with my hate for her for taking my child. The broken pieces of my life spread all around me and resonate from these walls.

The chance that I might run into memories of my past haunt me every day. I wake each morning with a prayer to God to help me make it through the day. Dear God, grant me the strength to keep my heart open, to forgive, and to let go of my past. Amen. I never know if I really believe my prayer bullshit.

I begin working at the family law office where Nancy got me the interview. My high school typing class comes in handy. I start work on the same day I interview; I guess I made a good impression. The office is in downtown Cleveland. It's easier to take the bus. Mom or Dad drop me off at the bus stop the first week, but by week two they buy me a small red two-door hatchback. I think they got tired of driving me around or my asking to use the car. I work four days a week, 9:00 a.m. to 4:00 p.m. I answer phones, set appointments, and assist the other full-time secretaries with court documents for five lawyers. It's a job, and I need to save some money for next year's school expenses. I board the bus at 7:45 a.m. in my small hometown of Beckville and travel to downtown Cleveland. It's a short thirty-minute bus ride on I-77 north. It gives me time to think, or to try not to think about, Levi, college, and how I am going to reclaim my freedom.

Levi calls when he can from basic boot camp training in Texas. His schedule is very busy, from what he can tell me during our brief phone calls. Fatigue heavy in his voice, I stay positive and try to lift his spirits. Our conversations surround my life, my summer job, my new car. He only wants to hear about what I've been doing, secretly checking to see if I am okay. Our weekly chats are a nice balm to my heart and leave me with a yearning to be loved, to love again, and share daily routines with someone. I support his journey and the task he has undertaken, knowing he's been forced to do whatever it takes to make ends meet while still reaching for his dreams. It's week six. Boot camp is going by fast, for me at least. I am not doing pushups at 5:00 a.m. or running ten miles a day in the hot Texas sun and humidity.

The workday is over. I swing open the door to the kitchen from the garage. Checking my watch, I calculate the time change between Levi and me, and I see it's just a few minutes past 6:00 p.m. in Texas. The home phone starts ringing. Sprinting down the hall, I toss my purse in the hallway. I don't want to miss this call; it could be Levi. He usually calls on Wednesdays, after he eats dinner. The new recruits get a few minutes of free time to use the phone. I usually plan to be home.

Lifting the receiver, I say, "Hello."

Levi's voice comes across the line with quick words and urgency.

"Jules, I got my transfer papers today."

Visions of Germany, England, and California enter my thoughts. I see castles, beaches, mountains, and the Berlin Wall. In our past conversations, we speculated about the cities, states, and countries where he could be stationed, based on the location the last graduating recruit class was shipped off to. Iceland, Alabama, and Japan.

"Do you want to know where I am going? Jules, do you hear me?"

I want to ask, "Did you see me? See me running after you?" But the answer haunts me.

So I say, "Yes, I hear you."

"I'm going to —"

I cut him off midsentence. "No, don't tell me," I blurt out. "You are better off without me. I need to figure things out, figure me out. Maybe I could come visit after you get settled, if you still want me to."

Silence lingers, putting his precious minutes at risk.

"Jules, come with me. I know I want you. I love you. I love everything about you. You are the only one who doesn't love you!"

Absorbing the words that have just filled my heart, I think, there he goes again throwing things out of my luggage.

Is that true? Pacing circles on the shag carpeting and making a racetrack in my room, I lose control on this speedway called life. With the phone pushed painfully against my ear, I stand there, frightened by the pain that love brings.

"The two hardest things for me to say are hello and goodbye because hello always leads to a good-bye somewhere down the road. I will miss you." The room spins out of control.

Sister, are all my hellos going to end in goodbyes?

"Jules, I have one more thing to tell you." His voice is strong and commanding. "*E kipa mai.* Jules, do you hear me? If you are ever ready to say hello again, promise me you will do this. Remember these Hawaiian words. E kipa mai. My time on the phone is up. I have to go." Click, dial tone playing in my ear, the phone goes dead.

Our connection severed, a part of me dies. Did I just say goodbye again? Scrambling for a tissue to wipe away the tears, I flop facedown on my bed, tossing the blanket over my head. What just happened? I was protecting myself. I didn't let him hurt me, so why do I feel so dismal. I won, didn't I?

⸙ ⸙ ⸙

I am drenched in sweat, drowning my dream of Adam in its tracks. Restless and afraid to close my eyes, I tell myself these reoccurring dreams of him must stop. Tossing, turning to escape the visions, I recall my most recent dream — me running for deliverance, only to end up at the front steps of church, with Adam standing there waiting for me. Restlessness is a torture and painfully pries my eyes open to stare into the darkness. I need to get out of this house; these walls echo my cries for help. The night is useless if you can't find peace. Kicking the covers off, I switch on the light and wait for some rays of sunrise.

What did Levi say? What were his foreign words to me? E kipa mai. Pacing, rubbing the back of my neck, I wonder how can I get a translation. The library! Throwing on a shirt and jeans, I head to the kitchen and brew a pot of coffee. Leaning against the counter, watching the coffee slowly fill the pot, I grab the telephone book off the shelf and start flipping through it to see if I can find out what time the library opens. It opens at nine o'clock on Saturdays. I slowly sip my black brew, impatient but trying to kill time before hopping into the car and heading out to do some research. I sure hope a library in Ohio has a book on Hawaiian language. I'm searching for a message in a bottle.

I pace outside the library, and my reflection follows me in the large glass panes. Wow, do I look disheveled. I could have at least flattened out my punk rocker bangs, which are sticking straight up. The doors will open any minute. I claw at my bangs to tame their outburst.

I peer inside, I follow the librarian's path inside, and she finally walks toward the door, keys in hand. She unlocks it and pushes it outward.

"Hello," she says, holding the door open for me. "You're here early. Are you looking for something specific?"

"Morning. Yes, I am looking for a language book. I am trying to find a translation of a word or phrase that is in Hawaiian. Do you think you could help me?"

"Let me put the keys back in the office, and then let's see what we can find. Meet me in the language aisle. That's the four hundreds."

I turn and survey the library and map out my direction. Before I make a move, she breezes past me and says, "Follow me."

I parade close behind her, footstep for footstep, until she stops halfway down the aisle. Her head moves and she talks to herself under her breath, scouring the books lined up by subject. She reaches up, pulls three books off the shelf, and hands them to me: *All About Hawaii*, *Travel the Islands*, and

Say it in Hawaiian. "Start reading. Hope you find what you're looking for. I would start with the top one."

"Thank you, or should I say aloha?" I smile as she walks away.

My hand skims across the cover of my new bible and its title *Say it in Hawaiian.* I open the hardback cover and read through the introduction pages at racer speed. Chapter One. The Hawaiian language has five vowels and only seven consonants: h, k, l, m, n, p, and w. **Are you testing me, Sister?** I skim the words on the pages, trying to make sense of this foreign language, searching for clues to solve this message from Levi. Chapter Two. Words that start with H. Hipa. Hipa means sheep. What the hell is he telling me about sheep? That can't be right. Digging in my pocket, I unravel my scribbled words on the paper. Kipa, not hipa. K. Fast forwarding to K, I scan down to "kipa." It means "to visit, come." Farther down the page I read, "See common Hawaiian phrases, Chapter Eight."

Hawaiian Words and Phrases to Express Love.

Aloha aula oe — I love you.

Aloha kaua — May there be love between us.

E hoomau maua kealoha — May our love last forever.

E kipa mai — Come to me.

As I cover my mouth with my hand, the words jump from the page: "English translation, meaning E kipa mai — Come to me."

I throw my head back in celebration and smile; the library light shines down on me like the Hawaiian sun. Blue Robe did tell me where he was going after all! He is in Hawaii. Slowly lowering myself to the floor, visions of Hawaii splash in my head. I close my eyes, and I envision the waves as they hit the sandy white seashore.

Kneeling, I let my fingers trace a pattern on the library carpet, and I pretend it's sand. *I could start over in Hawaii, Sister. Who couldn't be happy in Hawaii?*

🐚 🐚 🐚

Last night's dreams crash into real visions. Flash-backs from the unconscious keep reappearing when the sun has set and the evening crickets sing their songs. Shaking my head in disgust, the knives twist at my heart. I don't want to change the world; I just want change for me. What am I waiting for? At the age of nineteen, I am change.

I will leave this house that gives me nightmares, the repulsive town that whispers prayers behind their picket fences of lies. It's time. Unable to pretend anymore, I need to stop grieving, stop paying the price of love. I will end this dream, stop this grief, and start a new dream.

My friends didn't know it at the time, but they saved my life once. No one knew what I was going through in high school. My secrets and suffering were all mine. I didn't know if I wanted to live or die after the abortion. My friends loved me, loved me for me, and took care of me even though they didn't know I needed taking care of. Now it is time for me to save my own life. Save me from myself.

Sister Elizabeth, I'm taking charge from now on and leaving this house. Moving away from this small middle-class town in Ohio. This house with the long, straight concrete driveway, lined with towering pine trees that lead up to the house of stained bricks of danger orange and heavenly white, mortared together, holding in all the family secrets. The tall black iron lamppost shines light on the address numbers that welcome guests but shed no light on the darkened lies. Green-patterned carpeting lines the hallway to the three bedrooms, each filled with memories from the ones who slept in them. The painted walls hold all the love, lies, laughter, or hate, depending on which one is yours. Layers of colored paint seal in the sins so no one can see.

I reach for my phone, frantically pushing numbers, dialing my office's main line.

"Good morning, Radamorski, Rappaport, and Freedland," Claire, the office manager, says on the first ring.

"Morning, Claire, it's Jules. I have to quit." My own words even take me by surprise.

"Today, Jules? You want to quit today?"

"Yes, today. I'm sorry. I'm leaving town today; I just found out myself." A smile crosses my face

"Well, if you needed a few days off you could have asked." Claire sounds sympathetic.

"I don't plan on coming back, Claire."

"Hmm, okay. Thanks for calling, I guess. Bye, Jules. We are sorry to see you go. Good luck on wherever it is you're going."

"Thanks, Claire. I do need that. Bye."

Quickly ending the call before I change my mind, I rest the phone back on the cradle. I walk out to my car, open all the doors, and flip open the trunk. Returning to my room, I sweep my dresser drawer bottoms, fill my arms with clothes, and start loading my car.

Reckless at last. The action empowers me as I fill every crack and crevasse of my car with shoes, shirts, and jeans. And I might need a bathing suit, depending where I end up. I keep moving before I talk myself out of this decision.

What's the plan? My reckless plan is to drive west, west for sure. The long-term plan? Unknown. *Sister, get the road map out. Make new plans for me!*

The front seat is pushed all the way forward as I lean deep into the backseat. I look up and out through the hatchback. A car slows down to turn into the driveway and slowly approaches. I recognize it immediately. Marcella and Grace, my two older sisters, are sitting in the front seat. The conversation between them looks explosive, even from here.

Doors fly open. They're approaching my car at a fast pace, so I duck down in the backseat and peer out the window. They haven't seen me yet.

Our eyes meet out the rear side window, and they stop at my car, observing its contents. I slowly climb out.

"Jules, where are you going?" Grace asks.

"Claire from the office told your coworker you quit. She called me to see if you were okay. It was all news to me," Marcella says.

I don't know where I am going, so I say, "I'm driving west."

"West? What does that mean?" Grace says.

"You can't do this!" Marcella says, trailing behind her.

"Well, I am doing it, and I am doing it today." I turn away to get more stuff from the house.

"What about Mom and Dad? They won't be home for a week," Marcella says.

"I'm leaving today. I need change," I say.

"Change here. Go back to school in the fall. Get a new job," Marcella responds.

"I need change for two reasons: one, because I finally want to, and two, I'm hurting enough that I need to." My voice is back.

Both look at me with uncertainty for a few long moments, holding their bodies rigidly when I offer no deeper explanation about my reasons for leaving.

"I will leave Mom and Dad a note. It will be here when they return from their cruise," I say, easing their guilty consciences just a bit about letting me go.

I can hear it now: their youngest child left them. Their whispered hymns stifle the murmurs in church.

"We know we can't stop you, but we love you. We hope you change your mind. Don't hurt the ones who love you."

"I'm not the one throwing stones. I love you both very much."

As I retreat to the car, their heads shake in disappointment.

My red two-door hatchback is packed, bursting with hope, fear, doubt, and a lot of shoes. With both hands on the wheel, I back down the driveway. The car swings into the street, and I stop, slowly turning my head to look at my past, engraving the brick ranch house into my brain. With my fingers tapping on the wheel, I throw my shoulders back and sit up a little bit taller, fueled with power. I press the gas pedal, and the car accelerates forward.

My alter ego wants to see Adam one more time, and I fight with it. I need to move on. It's a painful thing to want to ask someone to love you, especially if they don't. A smile crosses my face; a snide giggle leaves my lips. It's a new day, new start. I settle for one last wave goodbye out my window, a sendoff. For the first time in a very long time, my mind doesn't listen to my heart—it leads me to the freeway, and my foot pushes heavy on the gas. With the windows down, the summer heat hits my face. I raise my arm out the window, gracing the skies with my middle finger. I feel only one thing: free. I am glad that the finger won.

Interstate 80 is my fast track west, filled with nothing but time, music, and open farmland. I'm mesmerized by the rolling hills of saluting corn planted in strategic straight lines for miles. Music and corn, music and corn. I turn the volume up, windows down, the Journey song entertains the corn on the open road. Warm, swirling air fills the car. I sing at the top of my lungs, knowing only the corn can hear my off-key tones singing about broken hearts.

The gas gauge slides toward the E — I'm at a quarter of a tank. The sign says fifteen miles to the next service station. I exit and fill the tank. I walk into the gas station to pay for my gas and discover Wendy's is conveniently inside, the smell of crispy French fries makes my stomach rumble with hunger. I place my order, grab my bag of steaming hot fast food, and head to the car.

I scour the glove box for my US map and unfold it, stretching it out over the hood of the car. With a cheeseburger in one hand, I slide the finger of my other hand across the paper map, tracing my path from my starting point, circling where I am now, planning my path ahead. My expedition has taken me through three states so far; they all start with the letter "I": Indiana, Illinois, Iowa.

Is this a sign? A hidden message on my map? "I" have made the right decision; it's finally about "I."

I throw away my cheeseburger wrapper, get back into the car, and head west on the open path to wherever I want, and I'm crossing out my "I's." The Wendy's Frosty and fries long gone, my car wheels continue to roll across another state border at a fast, smooth pace. The farther I flee from Ohio, the more I simply breathe, embracing uncertainty. Hope lives, finally creating a new path toward happiness. Deep down I know exactly where I am going.

My eyes grow heavy, the oncoming headlights blurring my crisp vision. I wiggle in my seat, and my butt awakes from sleeping. Shuffling side to side in my seat, I try to get some circulation in those cheeks. My headlights guide me off the freeway exit, and I roll to a stop at the end of the ramp, turning right into the parking lot of a Holiday Inn. I glance at my watch; it is minutes away from 11:00 p.m. I took Indiana, Illinois, and Iowa with a vengeance. I have been on the road for nineteen hours.

With my backpack over my shoulder, I lock my car, tossing my keys in the air and catching them with confidence. I walk into the empty lobby, pay cash for my room, grab my key, and head down the hallway to my room.

As I open the door, my hand grazes the wall for the light switch, throwing on all the lights. I check under the beds, in the closet, and behind the shower curtain before I return to lock and double lock the door. I slowly undress, peeling back the layers, piece after piece, leaving a trail of clothing to the bathroom. I turn the faucet all the way to hot and wait until the room fills with steam, creating a hazy landscape. The steaming water hits my body, pulsating on my aching muscles. I stretch my arms high over my head to release the heaviness in my limbs. Eyelids getting heavy, clouds of steam float above me while I drag the soap across my tired body. Inhaling the comforting scent of clean, I turn off the water, towel off, and crawl into bed. My wet hair soaks into the pillow as my naked body slides between the crisp white sheets. I close my eyes as the TV plays out the events of the day. Flashes of headlights dance all night on the wallpaper.

🐌 🐌 🐌

Colorado, Utah, Nevada all whiz by as the wind carries me west to California, the land of the setting sun. The LA traffic has me mystified about why so many people want to live here. I weave, crawl, speed down six sprawling lanes to Long Beach, CA. Three days of driving full force across the country, chasing the sun, chasing dreams into the sunset, night after night. I pull into the Port of Long Beach, shipping division. I've booked my car, filled with my only possessions, on the next cargo ship to Hawaii. I walk out of the office feeling accomplished and raise my hand to hail a taxi from the long line waiting outside the booking terminal office. After I throw my backpack onto the backseat, I slide in next to it and tell the driver, "LAX airport, please," and then whisper, "My final leg to a new beginning." At LAX, I scan the departure board. Hawaiian Air has a departure in two hours and fifteen minutes. I walk up to the ticket counter and am greeted with an "Aloha, checking in?"

"Yes. Well, no. I would like to purchase a one-way ticket to Honolulu today. There are seats for today's flight, right?" I clasp my hands together in prayer fashion.

"Yes, I will be able to accommodate you. Driver's license or another form of identification is all I need. And how will you be paying today?"

Handing my driver's license over the counter, I say, "Paying with cash." I pull my wallet out of my backpack and count my bills out on the counter. Two hundred dollars hits my savings hard, but it's a good investment toward happiness.

"Follow the corridor to terminal two. You will be leaving out of Gate 33," the ticket agent says.

"Thank you." I walk away, my one-way ticket in my hand.

I have not told Levi I'm coming. I haven't told anyone. I'm a little afraid. E kipa mai, I tell myself. Come to me.

Standing in front of the phone booth, I dig out the number Levi gave me from the bottom of my purse. With a deep breath, I push the numbers, not sure who it will connect me to.

I close my eyes. Ring, ring . . . before connecting. It's comforting to hear his voice. "Hello." Damn, it's an answering machine. "Hello, this is Levi. Leave a message."

My voice quivers, clearing my scratchy throat. "Hi . . . it's Jules. E kipa mai, I am coming. I land at 5:25 p.m. tonight, Hawaiian Air Flight 03. I will understand if you've changed your mind. Please don't come if you have." Quietly I place the phone receiver back in its cradle, ending the call, knowing I should have said more. I can always say more but never do.

I close my eyes and shake my head at my recklessness. What am I doing?

"Last call Hawaiian Air Flight 03 to Honolulu. All confirmed passengers need to make their way to Gate 33. Doors closing in five minutes."

Stuffing the number back in my backpack, I swing it over my shoulder and walk straight for the Jetway. *Sister, the sinner has a new address.*

🐾 🐾 🐾

I must have dozed off during the in-flight movie, all the driving having finally caught up with me. The piercing pitch jolts me awake as the pilot's voice echoes over the PA. "Prepare for landing. Cabin staff, please secure the cabin and take your seats for landing."

I cinch my seat belt a little tighter, press my forehead against the sundrenched window, and look at the fishing boats drifting in the deep waters of sapphire blue. The right wingtip seems to greet them as we bank above the Hawaiian coast. Pearl Harbor is off to the left as we make our final approach to Honolulu International Airport. The back wheel touches down on the runway, the burning rubber rolling across the heated pavement. My body tilts slightly to the right. Two wheels down, the nose lowers. Will he be here waiting for me? "Aloha, and welcome to the Honolulu International Airport. Please remain

seated until the seat belt sign is turned off. Mahalo."
I listen in disbelief; I am really in Hawaii.

On the edge of my seat, I stare at the seat belt sign, waiting for it to turn off. Ping. I am up, swirling my backpack around my back. My cheeks raise in a smile — I've made it to Hawaii, on my own, at the age of nineteen.

When I step off the plane onto the Jetway, I inhale the warm, salty air and walk steadily through the open-air airport terminal. The balmy temperatures bring a dewy glow to my skin. Below, in the courtyard, palm trees sway and gulping bright orange and yellow koi fish float in the water ponds. Muffled Hawaiian music echoes in the distance.

A sign points down on the escalator leading to the baggage claim. As I push the door open, the music is now crisp and clear. ALOHA, in big, colorful letters, is carved out of koa wood on the visitor sign. Hula dancers move their bodies to a live musical band.

I scan the crowd of people seeking out their loved ones. Homemade signs are held high to welcome friends, groups, and returning family back to the islands. Flowered necklaces drape from their arms as they wait to welcome someone lucky.

Slowly I walk, navigating through the crowd, tucking under and between signs, reading them as I go. ALOHA AUNTIE, WELCOME HOME MOM, RAINBOW ISLAND TOURS, BLUE ROBE MISSED YOU.

What? My cheeks flush, and I giggle with relief as the tingling shudders through my body. He is here—the sign gave it away. I walk toward him, and his shaved blond head peeks out from the corner of the sign with blue letters. His blue eyes follow.

"Jules." And then a whistle.

I smile at the familiar sound of the whiz between his lips.

After five thousand miles over freeways, through cornfields, lakes, rivers, and rolling hills, I am finally here and seeing him with my own eyes. I run the rest of the way to fill this gap between us, jumping into his arms, our bodies colliding and becoming one.

Caught off guard, he stumbles back, dropping the sign but not me. My feet are off the ground as Hawaiian music gently strums. Round and round he swings me. My toes sail above the floor. Throwing my head back, I feel the music, smell the salt air, enjoying this bear hug. Now *this* is something to remember. Our bodies mold together, and we stand cheek to cheek as I press closer to him.

This time I'm going to say "more" and not be silent, Sister.

"Hold me, hold me tight," I whisper into his ear. "Thank you for not wearing your robe. Thank you for being here. Thank you for being you."

His arms wrap tighter, holding me closer, and I nuzzle my face into his hair while inhaling deeply. "I missed the smell of your hair. I missed you. You are my heaven."

His lips cross mine with a gentle touch, and I place my head on his shoulder. His warm body intertwines with mine, warm breath heavy against my neck and ear. He whispers, "What do you say about taking a chance on me?" His soft, tender lips travel back to find mine.

I close my eyes to enjoy this moment, and I pray to God to give me the strength to move on and love again. Turning toward him, I hold his face in my hands, feeling his breath, this time kissing him back, this time with purpose.

He grabs my shoulders, pushing me away at arm's length, gripping tightly, as if he is afraid I will run, his eyes glued to mine. "E kipa mai. Marry me, Jules, marry me."

CHAPTER SEVENTEEN

Two weeks later, standing in our new bedroom, my knees trembling, I stare at my wedding dress hanging in the closet. Tomorrow is my wedding day. I've been told it's the best day of one's life. I should tell someone about my joyous day.

I never left a note the day I left the house like I told my sisters I would. The words were never right, not sincere; the virgin paper lay virgin white on the kitchen counter.

I procrastinated. Now guilt has won, and the irresponsible daughter number four needs to call home — my old home. Responsible for myself now, I should let them know my wedding is tomorrow. They should know where I am.

Pressure builds behind my eyes. My head pounds with pain, and I'm torn between tears of anger and happy wedding-day jitters. This phone call is the only thing standing in the way of leaving the past behind. Pacing back and forth around the bed, I finally stop. Reaching down, I grab the phone off the nightstand and start to dial.

Press one. My finger hovers over the button. Press two. I am dialing the only home phone number I have ever known. Press another one. My fingers quiver above the next number. I slouch forward, my head between my knees. My grip on the receiver is tight. With my other hand, I press my fingertips to my forehead to relieve the pressure in my head. It pounds, and the cyclone that whirls behind my eyes blurs the numbers on the phone. Forcing myself to sit up, I plant my feet on the cold tile floor for balance. Fingers move quickly, pressing the six, the five, the two, then hover over the last numbers.

This was a mistake. My other hand slowly moves to end this torturous call.

There's a soft knock on the door, and I look up to see Levi standing in the doorway, his arms crossed over his strong bare chest. It looks like he might have been standing there for a while.

"Jules, I didn't want to startle you. I'm right here for you if you need me," he says.

I stare at him. He stands firm and unwavering. He is my rock at this moment; he gives me strength. I nod my head up and down, whispering under my breath, "Yes, I need you."

I press the last two numbers. The slow drip of sweat travels down my cheeks, and I silently hope this connection over miles of ocean, followed by all the countryside, will misconnect, but it rings. I smile for a brief second while my mind thinks of mischievous things. I should have packed a few of those phones before I left. I tried calling home, Mom, really . . . no phones in the house. How odd! Hmm, wonder how that could happen.

"Hello." I'm five years old again, trembling at the sound of my mom's voice.

"Hi, Mom, it's Jules." I wipe my quivering lips.

"Dwayne, it's Jules. She's on the phone," she yells off into the distance.

"Mom, I'm in Hawaii."

"Dear God, how did you get there?"

"I'm with Levi. I arrived two weeks ago, and I am calling with news. Levi and I are getting married tomorrow."

"Jules, come home. Why are you getting married?"

"No, Mom." Long pause. "No. I am not coming home. This is my home now. Be happy for me."

"Don't do this to this family. Come home. Get married here if you have to," Mom whispers into the phone.

My throat is dry, and my mouth drops open as I gasp for air. It's happening all over again. I'm drowning in this conversation. The water is getting higher and higher; my words are boiling over.

"I don't have to get married, Mom. I want to."

My body convulses uncontrollably, my mind muddled with my past . . . with memories of being forced to go back.

"Goodbye Mom. Please tell Dad I love him. I will send pictures, I promise. Come visit if you want." Cutting her off, I sever the line between Hawaii and Ohio.

The phone drops to the tile floor, my shaking hand unable to hold onto it any longer. Clenching my fists, I dig my fingernails into my closed hands and squeeze my eyelids tight as I fall back onto the bed. Levi rushes to my side, cradling me until the shaking stops. I doze, and my mind goes to another place, a peaceful one, making room for Levi.

"Inhale . . . exhale . . ." he tells me, his arms nestled tight around my shoulders, nourishing me back to strength.

Opening my eyes, I briefly look up at the man holding me in my time of need.

"I will rise up to a better place, a better me, because of you."

"Close your eyes. Go to sleep. This day is over, and tomorrow is a new day, our wedding day. You'll be my Jules, forever and ever."

🐦 🐦 🐦

Levi stands next to the bed, motionless, calm. Slowly, I open my eyes. He is balancing a full cup of steaming hot coffee in his hands. I watch the cloud of steam rise from the cup and inhale the fresh aroma. My body perks up.

"Wake up, my love. It's our wedding day," he says.

Smiling back at him, I slowly sit up and gather the pillows behind me before leaning back, anticipating what's coming my way. As I stretch, I loosen any leftover tension from last night and reach my hand out for the coffee cup.

He pulls the blanket around me to keep me warm. "I love you," he says. "I want to be the one who brings you coffee in bed for the rest of our lives. I hope you feel that way, too."

Cradling the mug close to my face, I hope all those things are true and gaze at the steam rising to the heavens as if the future will somehow reveal itself there. "Yes, I do," I yell to him as he heads toward the bathroom to shower. "Today is the day we are getting married. You'd better look better than any groom in the whole building."

Levi made all the arrangements for us to be married at the courthouse by the Justice of the Peace. Sipping my coffee, I am amused by the title — we could all use a little peace. Springing out of bed, I try to lighten my mood. It is my wedding day, after all!

I startle Levi in the shower as I swing the door open to join him. Immediately his hands are eagerly working their way around my body, caressing my breasts. I slowly move his hands away, fighting off his continuous craving to touch me.

"Excuse me, mister. I'm getting married today — I can't be fooling around."

"I cannot help myself. I have a thing for single ladies about to get married."

After many failed attempts, he opens the shower door, turns, and gives me a long once-over before closing the door behind him.

Removing my rose-white dress from the hanger, I pull it over my head and slither the satiny silk down my body. It clings perfectly to the curves at my waist. The neckline dips down into a V, a feminine row of ruffles circles the short cap sleeves, and the dress flows to a finish just above my knees. Toes pointed, I slip my bare feet into my white sandals and fasten the strap around my ankles, noticing how tan my legs are from living in the Aloha State for only a few weeks.

Standing before the mirror, I hardly recognize this bride as I fasten the simple pearl earring studs behind my ear and put on a matching necklace to complement my wedding-day attire.

Levi emerges from the bathroom, dressed in his dark blue United States Air Force uniform, his accomplishments and awards pinned above his heart. Starched white shirt, blue tie, and hat complete his official uniform.

"Hey, good looking, can you fasten the clasp on my pearl necklace?"

He swoops in behind me, kissing my neck.

"Necklace, Levi!" I throw the pearls over my shoulder. "Those are some shiny shoes you got there, buddy. Can you lift those things up here so I can apply my lipstick? That reflection is blinding me."

He pretends to put me in a chokehold as I bend down toward his shoes. Laughter echoes down the hallway.

"Get in the car, bride. Let's go get hitched at the courthouse."

"Yes, sir," I say, saluting this handsome man in uniform.

🐜 🐜 🐜

We park directly across the street from the courthouse. As I gather coins for the parking meter, I wonder how long it takes to get married. One hour? Two hours? God forbid, this isn't a Catholic wedding. *Maybe you could be a witness, Sister Mary Elizabeth.* I smile, knowing that since I am living in sin I cannot even walk inside the Catholic Church, let alone get married in one.

Three quarters, three dimes, and four nickels later, Levi looks at the meter and shakes his head at my clumsiness. From behind his back, he pulls out one red rose and hands it to me. "For you, my love." The one rose that brought us together and keeps us together. Leaning into him, I place a soft kiss on his cheek, checking for lipstick residue before moving away.

Levi checks his watch, tapping on the glass face, and points at our destination across the street. "Jules, let's go. We can't be late. You can kiss me anytime you want after we are married." He rolls his eyes at me.

"No, don't say that. Someone else told me the same thing once," I blurt out. My heart sinks into my shoes, and my mind drifts off as I watch the cars whiz past me at high speed.

"Jules, can you hear me?"

"Yes." I try to gather my thoughts, to keep my wedding-day mood untethered.

We climb up the concrete steps holding hands, counting steps as we near the top. Looking up at the long row of glass doors, I see Sarah and Tim, our witnesses, waving just inside the doors to get our attention.

Levi's hand clasps mine as we walk through the glass doors to greet our friends. I try to muster up the same enthusiasm.

"Are you sure you want to witness this shotgun wedding?" I ask. "I've only known you a week."

"We're here for the drinks afterward! Just kidding. I would do anything for Levi," Tim says. "After going through boot camp together, we're like brothers."

Strangers parade past, leaning into our circle with whispers of congratulations. "Hey, congratulations to the bride and groom." Oblivious to my wedding costume, I look at them confused.

Oh yeah, the wedding dress.

"I'm not married yet!" I shout back, a smile pasted on my face. "My feet could get cold." I lean heavily into Levi's chest.

Scanning the long directory of names, office titles, and room numbers posted high on the wall, I scroll to the letter J, Justice of the Peace — Wedding Chapel, Room 208. Second floor. My gaze drifts to the stairs, and I try to feel exuberant, excited to start the new life ahead of me and leave the lies of the past behind. Over and over, I remind myself that my new life is ahead of me. The secrets and lies will all stay in the past.

I clench my one red rose between my fingers and swing around, searching for Levi's hand. Pulling it into mine, I hold it close to my chest and lead him across the lobby floor, heading up the stairs. One floor up we climb, two steps at a time. My dress flows behind me, the satin hem slapping Levi in the face. Sarah and Tim are in our wake, working their way up at a leisurely pace.

❧ ❧ ❧

The hallway is lined with one continuous wood bench, dark-stained, solid, judicial, strong. Lemon-scented furniture polish fills the air. Windows at eye level continue up the wall to the ceiling. I gaze at the trail of bench seats, and I try to maintain focus. Bench, windows, white walls, bench, windows, white walls. Cold metal industrial lights hang from the ceiling, an endless railway track. Glass windows to my left, closed office doors to my right. Walking fast down the white tiled flooring, we locate Room 208. The closed door bears a welcoming sign: TAKE A SEAT AND WAIT FOR YOUR NAME TO BE CALLED. We sit on the bench across from the closed wooden door and I stare at the white tile squares. My mind flashes to the waiting room with Adam. Next! I see myself sitting on the wooden bench, windows above my head, glass fogged over with the chill of the room. I can smell the bleach from the clean floors, my eyes watering from the scent. I am holding Adam's hand in the waiting room, waiting for my name to be called. "Next! Jules." I am in my hospital bed all alone. White. I see white. White sheets, white ceiling, and my white hospital gown with green triangles.

Levi breaks the silence as I stare into my past.

"Where would you like to eat dinner to celebrate? It should be special. It's our first meal as a married couple. You and I hitched. Hard to believe it's happening."

His question pulls me from my thoughts.

"Duke's? Fisherman's Wharf?" he asks.

Snickering, I bow my head and say, "How about Hawaii's world-famous Rainbow Drive-In?" I wait quietly for his reaction.

He laughs, smiles. "No, Jules! We are not having a plate lunch after we get married. You can have macaroni salad tomorrow."

The wooden door swings open, and a tall gentleman wearing a light blue Hawaiian print shirt appears and yells, "Next, Wong party."

A heavy sigh escapes my lips. "Whew," I whisper. Dropping the one long-stemmed rose Levi gave me, my head falls forward, and I gasp for air. Quickly, I glance around to see if anyone heard.

Thank goodness, all eyes are on the beautiful bride and the Wong party making their way toward the open door. The Wong party disappears as the door shuts behind them.

Relief invigorates my body. I gaze up at the rays of sunlight streaming in from the windows above, shimmering bolts of angelic sunlight floating in the air. It reminds me of church when I was a child, when the sun filtered through the sanctuary's stained-glass windows. Back then, I pretended it was angel dust clouds, the divine messenger floating above our heads.

Sister, I am marrying a man. Happy? I giggle to myself.

"Jules! Jules!" Levi is perched over me, caressing my hand in his.

"They called our name. Are you okay?"

Repeated blinking helps wash away the sting in my eyes from the smell of bleach. Shaking off his tender grip, I free my hand. Both hands grasp the smooth edge of the bench, my palms rubbing back and forth in rhythmic fashion over the curved edge in an attempt to calm myself. I push my body up; my heavy heart follows.

I stand. My feet too heavy to lift, I feel paralyzed. I stretch out my arm. Levi turns back and grabs it and guides me. *Click.* The door closes behind us.

Our escort pauses, waiting for our group to catch up. My toes tap, tap, tap on the tile floor, doing double-time. Together we stop and stand behind him as he points the way to the wedding chapel.

Following Levi's dizzy outline, I jerk to a stop. I catch a glimpse of glass vases filled with roses perched on tall pedestals at the altar. White, magical roses, symbolizing true love, the purest of flowers symbolizing spirituality.

"Levi, did you pick those flowers?"

"Yes, I hope you like them. Where is the rose I gave you?"

"I must have accidentally left it on the bench." Blood-red guilt runs through my body. He planned everything—everything for me.

Sarah and Tim are escorted ahead, and they are directed to stand next to the towering flower vases.

"Levi, please follow me. You'll be standing on the left, facing Juliette," the courthouse escort instructs him.

Softly, I correct him. "It's Jules, not Juliette."

"Juliette, I mean Jules, you stay here when you see Kimo," he says, pointing to the corner. "We'll start the music with the song Levi picked out, and you walk at your own pace to Levi."

Okay, but I have no idea what song Levi picked out.

Sister, give me the cue to go!

Levi drops my hand and heads toward the make-shift altar.

I stand alone.

Straight ahead, the Justice of the Peace, a stranger, makes eye contact with me.

He's not a priest, he's not a priest, I repeat to myself. I have no penance to say.

He nods hello and smiles in my direction. Nodding back, I click my heels together like Dorothy.

The nod must be a signal to Kimo, the music man. The room comes alive at the first touch of the piano key, the soft tones echoing in my ears. I slowly walk toward Levi, passing by three rows of empty seats to music that almost sounds familiar. Turning, I look first at the man who is going to marry us. Then I turn to Levi, the man I am marrying. His eyes are glued to me as if he knows I want to run away.

"Let's begin. Juliette and Levi, please join hands. Welcome all who have gathered here to witness this special event."

I chuckle out loud, and Levi gives me a serious raised-eyebrow look. The Justice of the Peace is mouthing words, but I am still giggling at his first sentence. I stare into Levi's eyes, searching for some common ground to bring my attention back to this serious moment.

He loves me. I can feel it in his gentle touch on my hands, holding them like he owns them, grasping them tightly in a secure way. As he gently rubs his thumb over mine, his blue eyes search for clues, a look of puzzlement on his face.

Oh my God. I'm getting married! What am I doing?

My heart pounds louder; it echoes in my ears. My knees feel weak. Sweat drips down my cleavage.

It's just nerves, right? Do this, Jules! Marry him. Be happy. You deserve to be happy. Look how he loves you. Look back at him. He fought for you, fought to keep you. No one else has ever done that.

The Justice of the Peace says, "Is there anyone here who has any reason to object to this unity of marriage between Levi and Juliette?"

No, not Juliette again. Juliette is not here.

Praying for a miracle, I look to the back of the room and then back to Levi.

Adam, come and take me away. Memories come bubbling to the surface. I see Adam, his hand stretching out for me to take it. I want to take it; I want to go with him. The back door to the chapel opens, squeaking oh so slowly. I quickly searching the faces entering. Is it Adam?

The next wedding party tiptoes into the room, quietly lowering themselves into the last row of seats. My head drops forward. I wipe the visions of Adam from my mind, and I am quickly brought back to reality, my white wedding sandals looking back up at me.

It is not over for Adam and me. I am not done loving him, longing for him with intoxicating desire. I cannot love Levi the way he deserves to be loved. I have not forgiven Adam or myself. I have not found my inner peace. Levi deserves more, more than I can give. I cannot marry him.

The demanding voice of the Justice of the Peace overtakes my thoughts. My focus returns, and I see the man standing across from me smiling handsomely in his Air Force uniform.

"Levi, do you take Juliette to be your beloved wife, to have and to hold, to be at her side in sorrow and in joy, in the good times and the bad, and to love and cherish her for all the days of your life?"

Please say *no*, you don't want to marry me. Please . . . please . . . please.

Without hesitation, with joy in his voice, Levi says, "I do." His blue eyes piercing mine, he smiles and squeezes my hands in confirmation of his love for me.

"Do you, Jules" — he finally says my name correctly — "take Levi to be your beloved husband, to have and to hold, to be at his side in sorrow and in joy, in the good times and in the bad, and to love and cherish him for all the days of your life?"

My heart pounds faster. No, no, no. I rehearse the words in my head. Someone please object to this marriage. I search the crowd now gathered at the back of the room. *Sister, are you back there?*

I spot the exit sign illuminated above the door and mentally calculate the distance from here to there. Standing at the starting line, I swallow and my throat dries with guilt. On three, the gun goes off in my head, my mouth drops open, and the air whistles deep down into my throat. I need to make the right choice for Levi and me, to find peace and tranquility in my heart. My feet are set to run; my eyes likely look dark and serious. My breathing is slow and even . . . "I do."

We head out the door hand in hand, down the steps, and run to the car. Glancing at the parking meter, I let a laugh escape my lips, and I yell across the car to Levi, "We have the Catholic Church beat. We overpaid. There are seventeen minutes left on the parking meter."

CHAPTER EIGHTEEN

*T**hree years later . . . Seattle, Washington.***
Slamming the back door of the car shut with my foot, I balance my groceries in my arms as I head toward the house. I juggle the bags from arm to arm, finally lining the key up with the lock on the door. I stumble up the step, tripping into the kitchen. With aching arms, I lift the bags onto the counter. My purse starts vibrating: my pager. I shift my shoulders forward and back until my purse swings within reach. Reaching into the bottom, I grab my pager and glance down at the screen. It's an Ohio number — my sister Grace.

I go into the living room to call her.

"Hello, Grace, what's up? What's going on?"

"Jules, you need to come home!"

"What? Why?"

"Mom and Dad are throwing a twentieth wedding anniversary party for Marcella and Ken in three weeks, and she mentioned to me she wished we could all be together."

"I cannot come. I cannot get time off from flying. I don't have vacation." Excuses roll comfortably from my lips.

"Mom wants us all together. It would mean a lot to her. You and Levi, maybe you two can come for a short weekend. Please."

"Levi's not coming," I say, wiggling out of my coat as I juggle the phone ear to chin. My body heats up. My coat drops to the floor. I'm filled with information overload and overheated. Tension builds. Grabbing the back of the chair, I hold on for stability, then swing my body into the solid seat. The vault of emotions is opening: that town, that room, my old house. People's faces flash before me and sweat drips inside my bra line.

"I am not coming." My voice gets louder. "Levi is not coming. We are not coming."

Silence is my friend at this moment, and I slip in a quick prayer to the Sister for guidance. Words stop traveling through the phone lines. Grace is quiet; I am quiet.

She doesn't know about Levi. I didn't tell her or anybody in my family. I failed. I failed him. Visions of his face appear before me, his blue eyes smiling up at me, begging for me to love him.

Grace waits on the other end of the phone line for my answer. How do I work that into our conversation? *Sister Elizabeth, the sinner has a lot of explaining to do.*

"Jules, are you still there?" Grace's voice jerks me into real time.

The silence is broken. Thoughts of Levi still play in my head, and I rub my arms to remind myself of the sand he grinds into my skin.

"Jules, Mom is sick. She has been for a few months. I didn't want to have to tell you over the phone. You should come home; she is not getting better."

My eyes swell, and years of tears roll uncontrollably down my cheeks. Are they for me or for Mom? I squeeze my eyes, trying to shut off the stream, but the tears continue dropping into my lap. Choking on my tears, I hiccup my question.

"What kind of sick?"

"Doctors have another MRI scheduled. It's brain cancer, Jules. We will know after the next tests whether the chemo and radiation treatments have made some headway, but it's not looking positive; she's not getting any stronger."

"Why didn't you call me sooner? This sounds bad, really bad."

"It is, Jules, it is."

My mind plays Grace's words over and over. Can I say no? No, I am not coming to see Mom? There was a funeral in that house a long time ago, I think, remembering the wallpaper on the dining room walls. It was mine. I rose from the dead. I survived. Could I be going back to make plans for hers? I can do this — go back to that house, that town, face the past, make peace, wash away the shame. I can drop the baggage I've been carrying once and for all. I will find the courage to do this, courage that I have earned through my years of being free.

Throwing my shoulders back, I stand up and look in the mirror across the room. I look strong. I am strong. I can do this.

"Yes," I say. "I will come home." Correcting myself, I say, "I will come to Ohio."

CHAPTER NINETEEN

Two days later, I sit behind the wheel of my car, my bags next to me. "Start the damn car," I say out loud. My fidgety fingers twist the key. The sound of the engine purrs. I put the car in reverse and slowly start to back out of the garage. My foot hits the brake. *Stop.* I rest my head on the steering wheel, whispering under my breath, "Just go to Ohio, forgive and move on. I had a great childhood; I love Mom. Go, Jules, just go."

Still in prayer position, I say, "God have mercy on me," and I feel my courage return. **Sister, just so you know, I've got this!**

Forty-five minutes later, I pull into the parking garage at the Seattle-Tacoma airport. I glance at my watch, grab my bag, and walk with fiery determination to my gate.

With my feet, I maneuver my leather carry-on under the seat in front of me. Settling into my seat, I listen as the pilot announces the flight time to Cleveland. Exhaling all the air from my lungs, I take a deep breath in through my nose. Yoga breathing — in and out — trying to relax. My thoughts travel to Levi, and I remind myself to call him when I get to the house.

I rest my head against the window. The engines roar as we gain speed down the runway. Reaching down, I tug one more time to tighten my seat belt. I inhale deeply through my nose, exhale deeply through my mouth, and keep saying that word to myself: runway, runway. Runway should be my middle name. How am I going to tell them Levi is not with me? As the plane jettisons through the clouds, I silently pray to find some answers as we climb toward heaven and closer to God.

As the white clouds float by, thoughts of Levi tug at my heart, and I replay the day he floated out of our marriage.

Levi and I were a young couple going through the motions until my heart's yearnings for my first love could no longer be suppressed under my protective armor. Levi tried to pleasure me into loving him, devouring my body and entertaining my mind, hoping to see my face light up again. You can try to fool your mind, but you can't fake it when your body dreams of being pleasured by another. Levi slowly came to know mine did. The words he said to me cut deep into my heart with the sharpness of their truth. It was the last night we lay together, his strong arms draped around me, his warm breath wafting through my hair as he calmly whispered in my ear. I play his words over again in my head, "Jules, I have pressed up against you, night after night, wanting to keep you warm and safe. I loved you with loyal devotion. I want to hold you like this forever, love you forever, together forever. I wish your heart felt the same. I know it doesn't. You are somewhere else. You are not here with me, and this kind of love hurts."

"Levi," I said, trying to stop him from talking anymore.

He told me to not talk anymore. I stopped and just listened.

"I want to occupy your mind, but I don't. Your mind and body are occupied by someone else. I want you to love me, hold me, want me. I don't think you can ever do that."

Tears rolled down my face, falling over my cheeks, settling in a pool of sorrows on my pillow. Words couldn't fix this; words were not the answer. We both knew I couldn't love him like I should.

Tears continued to flow, for me because he was leaving me, for him because he deserved to be loved, especially by me. Reality set in like sand grinding against skin, the small, fine granules reminding me of what a broken heart feels like. Levi — forever my sand, never to be brushed away. *Sister, thank you for bringing Levi into my life. I will never forget how I hurt him by not loving him.*

I filed for divorce one week later and moved to Seattle a single woman, with no one to blame but myself. I ran from being loved, chasing the magical love my heart was not ready to let go of.

๛ ๛ ๛

The late afternoon sun fills the sky as the wheels touch down at Cleveland Hopkins Airport. I rent a car and drive to my old house. It is the end of summer, and the afternoon heat follows me as I walk to the back-porch door, blooming flowers lining the path. A note taped inside the screen door says: Be back soon, Mom had doctor's appointment. Signed, Mom and Dad. I pull the well-worn red key from my pocket, pretty sure it will work after all these years. Stepping over the familiar threshold, a chill crosses over my body: it all looks the same. Cautiously I turn the corner, pausing before I enter the kitchen to check for the trailing wallpaper. I quickly scan the rest of the room; it is all the same. The phone mounted on the kitchen wall reminds me that I need to call Levi. His phone number fresh in my mind, I smile as I dial the ingrained numbers. It rings only once before it goes to voicemail. His voice is sweet and soft.

"Hi, Levi, it's Jules. I was hoping to talk to you. I am home," I say, stuttering at the sound of my words. "Not home." I clear my throat. "Ohio. I'm going to tell them about us. Mom is sick—that's why I'm here. Call me later if you want to talk. Forever sorry."

I collapse on the family room floor, my mind unwinding from my cross-country flight. Returning home all grown-up empowers me. I laugh nervously while I run my fingertips over the green shag carpeting, moving my angel-wing arms up and down. The sun streaming through the window onto my body feels luxurious, and I enjoy the late summer heat. A few moments alone are just what I need. I relish the calm and quiet that surrounds me.

I must have dozed off as the vibration of the garage door opening beneath me startles me awake. I lie still, unsure of what's about to happen. The door swings open and Mom steps into the room. My heart beats faster at the sight of her fragile, shortened body. Walking slowly toward her, I wrap my arms around the skeleton figure and kiss her cheek.

"Hi, Mom."

Then swinging briskly around, I hurl myself at Dad, jumping into his welcoming arms. "Daddy, I missed you." I tug on his sleeve.

We huddle close, locking arms as we move toward the kitchen. Mom is working her way into a chair at the head of the kitchen table.

"Jules, we could have picked you up at the airport. We didn't know what time you would be here."

"Mom, I rented a car. It was just easier."

"I heard from Grace you moved to Seattle. The airlines have been good to you. Do you still fly to Hawaii?"

"Yes, Mom, I still fly to Hawaii, but my home is in Seattle now. I got a transfer. I love my job as a flight attendant."

"Dwayne, get her something to eat. I got you poppy seed donuts and stuffed cabbage. I know those are your two favorites."

"I'll get it, Mom. Dad, sit down, please." I pause for a brief second. "Mom, Levi's home is still in Hawaii. Who wants some stuffed cabbage? Dad, should I warm some up for you?"

Mom says, "This is your home. Your room is all made up for you. It hasn't changed much since you . . . left. Be sure to eat. There is a lot of food in the refrigerator from the neighbors."

No reaction to Levi and me living apart. With a heavy sigh of relief, I tuck my head inside the cool refrigerator, pull out a casserole dish, and prepare a plate of food for Dad. I'm sure I will hear about it later.

Mom fills me in on which neighbor was nice enough to drop off which casserole or dessert. Fond memories of each of them emerge as she says their names. She rates each food item like a food critic, not by her taste buds, but by Dad's. She has not been able to eat because of the chemo and radiation treatments. I realize Grace was telling the truth, Mom has been sick for a while. I'm riddled with guilt for not coming sooner. Illness has affected her body but not her spunky ability to make fun of her friends' cooking. Dad is the final food judge, which is comical. He is the type of man who's never judged anyone or anything. The gentlest of men, sweetest of heart, with never a complaint in his calm world of words and gestures.

Moving around the dining room, reading random notes of kindness from neighbors and friends, I realize there have been many prayers and much caring for our family.

Dad eats everything I warm up, enjoying it and indicating his pleasure. "Mmm," he says more than a few times. Mom is telling me where each dish came from. I listen, jotting down what each neighbor cooked or baked and dropped off for the family.

"Jules, in the morning, can you write thank-you cards for me to all those people and hand deliver them to everybody? They are just going to be tickled to see you, and then could you pick up my prescriptions on the way back home?"

"Of course, Mom." She shakily pushes away from the table and walks out of the kitchen down the hallway.

"I'm going to bed. Good night, remember tomorrow we will write thank-you notes, Jules."

"Got it, Mom. We will first thing"

"Before I forget, you need to be home from running errands by three o'clock. The doctor's office said they would call with results from the last MRI. Jules, make sure you are home by then."

"Yes, I will be. I'll be sure of it. Night, Mom. Thank you for the donuts and stuffed cabbage. You were right, they are my favorite."

Dad and I finish our dinner, splitting a poppy seed donut and talking about Las Vegas, Hawaii, Seattle, and my travels.

"Glad you came home. I don't get poppy seed donuts anymore." Dad smiles, and then finishes his last bite.

Together, we let our laughter fill the room. I guess I am home.

"Thanks for cleaning up, Jules," Dad says at last. "I'm going to bed." He puts his dishes in the sink.

The sun is setting on this day, making way for the next. Slowly I walk down the hallway to my bedroom, suitcase in hand. My fingers trace the walls to my room at the end. Out of habit, I check behind me to see if Mom can see. When I was young, I would have heard, "Get your fingers off the walls, Jules." I turn on the overhead ceiling light in my room. I remember Christmas mornings in my pajamas, smelling Thanksgiving turkey cooking in the oven, and Fourth of July parties in the backyard. I stand in the doorway, gazing at the shag canary-orange carpeting that connects with the yellow painted walls. Dad let me pick the color. I giggle at the memory. Then I look up to see the hairline crack in the ceiling — still there.

Dropping my suitcase, I walk over to the night stand; the phone is back. Slowly pulling down the covers, I crawl into my bed, the same one I used to sleep in when I was a child. I pull the covers over my head, anxiously exhaling; nothing has changed, except the room changed me. Seconds pass. I peek out from under the sheets and reach for the phone lying in its cradle. I grasp it all in my hand, clutch it hard to my chest, and let out a sigh of relief, finally resting, drifting off to sleep.

It's 1:52 a.m. and Mom is restless. I hear shuffling back and forth to the bathroom, pacing in the hallway, moaning in the night. Not sure of what to do, I lie in bed and pray for her. I ask God what life lesson this is. I do not like this lesson. I'm not strong enough to see my mother sick or weak.

I must have dozed off. The clock reads 9:42 a.m., and with the three-hour time change, it's time to get up. After dressing for my day, I head for the kitchen for a much-needed cup of coffee.

"Sit here, Jules. The cards are ready." Mom hands me a big mug of black joe.

The strong aroma breathes new life into me, and I slowly sip the hot, steamy brew, forcing my body to wake up.

Mom's been up for hours and is ready to start. "Mrs. York brought lasagna, homemade cookies, and lemon squares. You got that, Jules?" As she stands over me, I notice her clothes hanging loosely from her body.

"Yes, Mom. I haven't seen Mrs. York in years." Guilty by my own admission.

"Now Mrs. Bobich, she's quite the cook, must be the Italian in her. Here are my notes on what she brought over." Mom pushes her pad of paper over to me.

"Got it, Mom, but isn't she Polish? I will finish them all and drop them off." I gulp down more coffee, followed by a bite of another donut.

𓂃 𓂃 𓂃

I return home in plenty of time, quickly sharing some of the conversations and well wishes that were sent Mom's way.

"Mrs. York could hardly believe it was me. It was a nice surprise. Saw Mr. and Mrs. Bobich too."

"And Mrs. Ricardo, was she home?" Mom asks. "She's always doing something."

"No, I left the thank-you note in her mailbox."

I return to my room and all is calm until the phone rings.

"Jules, pick up the phone and answer it." My mother's voice travels down the hall.

"Hello? Hello, Dr. Russell, one moment, please." I open my bedroom door, phone in hand. Covering the mouthpiece, I yell, "Mom, Dad, it's Dr. Russell. Pick up the other phone."

Mom and Dad are sitting together in the family room. I put the phone back to my ear and hear the other receiver pick up, so I know Mom and Dad are on.

I say, "Good afternoon, Dr. Russell. There are three of us on the line. Doris, Dwayne, and my name is Jules, one of their daughters." Sliding my pad of paper around, I click the top of the pen on and off with a nervous twitch.

He responds, "That's excellent. The more ears that hear the message, the better. Unfortunately, I do not have good news. The radiation and chemo treatments did not shrink the tumor. The results from our last MRI are in, and the tumor has grown, it is growing at a very aggressive rate. Glioblastoma multiforme."

Sounding it out in my head, I jot it down on the paper.

"The form of cancer that you have is the most aggressive in the brain. We were hopeful we could slow it down, but that was not the case. There is no known cure right now. There is promising research underway, but not soon enough for us."

What? I'm screaming in my head. I want to hang up. I want to run.

The doctor continues to talk. "I'm sorry to say that, in my medical opinion, all radiation and chemo options have been exhausted. But if you want a second opinion, I can get you some names."

I listen now with deaf ears, dropping my pen on the floor, notes no longer needed.

"I cannot predict how much longer you will live, but you do have a terminal illness. We have ways to help with pain and suffering, and I will be here for you. We all die as we live. I can only recommend that you try to enjoy each and every day you have together. I am sorry to deliver this devastating news. I will have hospice contact you to make sure they offer the services you may need to make things as easy as possible. Please call me if you have any more questions after this all settles in."

Mom says, "Goodbye."

"Thank you for calling, Dr. Russell," I say, and slowly lower my phone to the cradle. Crippled by the news, I grab my pillow and put it over my mouth. "Fuck you, cancer," I scream.

Mom and Dad were on speakerphone in the family room. We're in different parts of the house, thinking different things, wishing it all were different.

Picking myself up off the bed, I gather my courage, dragging my hurting heart all the way down the hall to find Mom. I enter the kitchen, hurrying to find a seat at the dinner table before my legs give way.

"I'm going to finish the dishes," Mom says. "Jules, you can dry them and put them away."

With my shoulders slouched, my eyes fill with ocean water ready to crash down on the beach. I stand, move next to Mom, and pick up a dish towel, drying the dishes while wiping away my rolling tears.

Mom taps me on the head with her wet hands and says, "We have a party to go to tomorrow. Finish up and let's go over the details for the party . . . and keep your fingers off the walls."

I let out a tearful laugh. "Okay, Mom."

CHAPTER TWENTY

Two weeks later, I am again sitting in the living room of my Ohio home. That's right — I couldn't stay away, not this time. The tables have turned. I returned to my parents' home after a brief respite, searching deeply within. I can't heal myself without helping to get my mom healed. I love her. She isn't asking for my help; she is helping me remember what love is between a mother and daughter. No script is written on parenthood. We're all doing the best we can.

Taking a quiet break on the couch is our new normal routine. With no rules, no time zones, twenty-four hours has a new meaning. Sunsets bring restless nights. Mom calls out into the darkness, "Jules, Juliette, Jules."

Struggling somewhere between being asleep and awake, I jump to my feet, running like a drunken thief to reach her before she wakes Dad.

"Mom, I'm right here. What do you need?"

"Water, my water glass is empty. Can you find some Vaseline for my dry lips?"

"Yes, Mom," I say sheepishly. After filling her water cup, I place the Vaseline tin within reach. I gaze down.

Her withering limbs seem to be losing strength every day. "Anything else?" I tuck the covers back around her neck.

"No. Sorry to wake you. Go back to bed."

"Mom, never be sorry." I tiptoe back to my bed, pulling the covers over my head to shield me from the fear of sickness.

No one in this family is ready to say it, but the reality is we are losing Mom. The mom who used to spoon-feed us is now spoon-fed. The mom who used to drink coffee by the mugful now drinks with straws. The mom who used to gallop throughout this house is now confined to her stable and uses a bedpan. They say you must hit rock bottom before you can climb back up. Has Mom hit rock bottom, or is it I who have hit rock bottom?

Settling into our positions in the family room, I fold my body in half, molding it to fit into the pint-size couch, wrapping the Christmas-colored afghan around me. Mom sits in her new recliner lift chair. I pile blankets around her to keep her disappearing body warm. Mom starts talking while I shift one more time to get comfortable in my spot. I am trying to concentrate, but I'm caught up in my own emotions about her declining physical appearance and the struggle she just had getting into her chair. The simplest things are not so simple anymore. Did I eat today?

"Mom, you hungry? Want me to get you something?" The smell of chicken soup on the stove makes my stomach rumble.

"No." She keeps talking. "Remember all the car trips we took to Massachusetts?"

"Yes, Mom, I remember the long car ride. It was really long. I was crammed in the backseat."

I bring myself back to the conversation. There will come a time when I'll replay these stories over and over again for the rest of my life. These stories are Mom's, and she must feel the need to say these words . . . to tell the stories, to reminisce about the vacations on the beaches of North Carolina, clam-bakes in Nantucket, the silly places we stopped along the way in South Dakota.

My mind stamps the details of this small room painted in green. Green is the color of spring, new growth, vitality. I glance back at Mom, recording her voice in my head so I never forget. She goes on and on about her memories of me and my sisters growing up: dating, driving, and prom dresses.

Her words vibrate off the walls. "Yes, Mom, I re-member where we stopped in South Dakota." The smell of chicken noodle soup is still on my mind. I yell, "Dad, soup is on the stove, it is ready. Can you turn it off?"

Feathery rays of sunlight stream past me onto the family room floor as the setting sun moves west. My mind relaxes in the summer memories of my sister and I doing cartwheels across the front lawn. I listen to Mom's raspy voice.

I keep my eyelashes padlocked shut and squeeze away my mental fatigue. I clear my throat, hoping it will improve my hearing. Did I miss something? She is no longer talking about vacations? Suddenly, I'm jolted by her voice, her words floating in the foggy air.

What did she just say? Did she say his name? The name not spoken in this house? Forbidden words about what happened? Blinking repeatedly, I struggle to register her words. What is happening? It's getting harder to breathe; more toxic air fills my chest as she continues to talk. My vision grows blurry, and the room starts to spin out of control. In a soft, shallow whimper, I say, "Mom, please stop."

She doesn't hear my cries for her to stop — to stop talking. She says his name again.

"Adam, remember him, Jules?"

Strong, sharp, contractions rattle in my stomach, the contents of my insides working their way up. I swallow hard to push everything back down. Remember him? Of course, I remember him. I've been trying to forget him for what seems like my whole life.

Why is Mom talking about somebody I used to know, somebody I used to love in my other life? I can't breathe. Sweating from the inside out, I'm raw, my scars exposed. As I sit up, my fingers dig into the fabric of the cloth couch. Her voice still echoing with words from the past, I turn and face her

I feel as if my blood is boiling, racing through my body. My face heats up, my stomach churns with bile. Shaking, I dig my fingers deeper into the couch. The room grows bright and the setting sun hits my face. The clouds outside the windowpane disperse. I'm struggling with mouth and brain to say his name. My mouth is dry, my lips moving, mouthing "A-D-A-M." Chest rising, I inhale through flared nostrils, exhale, close my eyes, and pray for strength as tears roll down my cheeks.

I can see him, his face close to mine; his deep brown eyes tranquilize me. Lifting my arm, I reach out, and my fingers gently touch his face. I run my fingers through his short black wavy hair. My lips turn up. Slowly, I trace his lips, and the softness of his velvet skin electrifies me. As I inhale deeply, the sweetness of his body fills my lungs. My shoulder blades flexing like wings, his warm breath on my face travels down my neck. His soft lips glide over my eager skin, down my shoulders. We pause, his lips barely touching mine, wanting more, craving more. I squeeze my eyes tighter, enjoying the calming pleasure of finally being together again. I lift my arm to put it around his neck, preparing to kiss his soft lips.

"I love you," I whisper. "Always have."

I slowly open my eyes. I sober up to see Mom's wheelchair looking back at me. He is not here. He left me, left me behind, and never looked back at the sinner. *Sister, my mind is playing games on me. Please help me.*

Mom's still throwing daggers with her words. "He never loved you. He got you pregnant and left."

Stomping my feet down like a bomb on the floor, I stand. Her vicious words have just detonated my life again. Dragging the dead weight of my shattered body, I move slowly, staggering forward to escape this minefield of killing words. My heart shell-shocked, I enter the living room, out of sight of Mom, but her voice still bounces off the walls.

"I protected you from him — that's what mothers do."

I collapse to my knees, dropping hard onto the carpeting; the rug burns me to an abrupt stop. Her words paralyze me, and my head free-falls to the floor. Resting the top of my head on the carpet, I cover my head with my arms to quiet the room. What just happened? What hit me? Run, run. Run away. Get up. Get out of here.

Conflict in my head, the pressure on my temples blurs my vision. I'm lost in regurgitated emotion, unable to stand. On my hands and knees, I crawl down the dark hallway to my room. My voice crackles from the noose around my neck as I let out a yell. "Dad, I'm going to bed."

§＆ §＆ §＆

Shutting the door behind me, I scramble to a stand and dash toward my suitcase. I throw it open, and in one fell swoop I grab the clothes hanging in my closet, wire hangers still attached. I push against the top forcefully until it zips shut. I crawl into bed, still wearing my clothes. *Sister, was this your plan? Opening my life, abruptly zipping it wide open, reliving my hidden secrets and old wounds?* My past life and the secrets that jolted me awake have collided. This time I can choose to run or choose to face them.

History is repeating itself. My face is pressed firmly into my pillow; my breath is hot on my cheeks. Heart beating at double speed, I flash back to another time in this bed, alone in this room. I sit up and grab the phone while glancing at the phone jack on the wall. I can change my history.

"Hello, you have reached Continental Airlines, can I help you?"

"Yes, hello. I would like to change my reservation. My name is . . ." This time, I will save myself.

My alarm goes off at 3:00 a.m., and I arise in the darkness of the moonlight hours. I grab my suitcase and purse and tiptoe down the green shag carpeting, stopping in the kitchen to scribble a note:

Dear Dad,
Sorry I had to leave. Be back soon.
I love you. Call soon.
Jules

The cold air is refreshing as I step onto the front porch. Carrying my heavy heart, I escape this house once again.

CHAPTER TWENTY-ONE

I have been gone for two weeks, and a lot has changed. First, I didn't know if I was going to return, but I am here. Mom has hit rock bottom and so have I. Life lesson today: define rock bottom. Mom has accepted her withering body will not recover — that is her rock bottom. She is not getting better; she will die soon. I have accepted I am dying unless I deal with my past, accept it, and move on. Maybe that's why I'm here. *Sister, you work in mysterious ways.*

This could be a monumental moment in time. Our lives have something in common: death and dying. How unfortunate that dying is what it took to bring Mom and me back together. Two lives dying two different deaths. I have been dying on the inside with an unrepaired broken heart, invisible to all. Mom is dying from a disease that breaks your heart, visible to all.

I still sleep at the house that I grew up in, but Mom no longer does. It gives the word "home" a whole new meaning, or does home just need a new definition? Is home where your family sleeps? Is home wherever you place your heart, calmed by whom you choose to spend your life with?

The plans have been in the making since I last left, but it has finally come to the point that we can no longer take care of all of Mom's needs at home. She has moved into a hospice care facility. It is a beautiful, brand-new building off the shores of Lake Erie in Cleveland, Ohio. The solid brick single-story building has wide hallways and private rooms for patients to die in the presence of family and friends. There's a chapel to make those last-minute pleas to your God for forgiveness and for a peaceful entry to heaven; an art room to take your thoughts off the dying and to entertain the mind with beautiful art; and a family room with a play area for children who are visiting dying grandparents, mothers, and fathers. The naïve are the lucky ones, I think to myself. Even if it's temporary.

The moment I step through the glass double doors of the entrance, smiling faces, warm hearts, and people with amazing souls greet me. It's almost a first taste of heaven. I can only wish that my soul could be as open to the sick and dying as the nurses' souls are. Selflessness and love pour out of each of them like water flows from a faucet. They don't judge, favor, or doubt the living souls they are caring for, and they make it feel like it's a privilege to take care of the living until their very last breath. I am adjusting to not just coming to see my mom when I visit her; I am now visiting a whole building of patients who are not only sick but also dying. I am visiting the dying.

Conversations do not include "What you will be doing next week?" "Any vacations planned?" because next week is a maybe when you are fighting for one more day, one more hour, or your next breath. I never again mention his name on my visit. It really doesn't matter. Or does it? We just never discuss it again. Dying decisions are being made. We adjust to different surroundings, schedules, and lack of privacy. I'm forced to learn a lot about myself and patience, or lack thereof. The healthy living thrown into this world of the sick and dying. One day does make a difference.

Kissing Mom on the cheek I say, "See you in two weeks, I have to head back to work."

"Okay, see you soon." Mom says.

CHAPTER TWENTY-TWO

At the end of my shift, my flight back to Seattle is on time. I board my plane in Los Angeles and settle into my passenger seat, unwinding from my day serving passengers. My flying day is over as a flight attendant. With my book open on my lap and my headset on, I climb out of the crowded LAX skies and head for the forest green state of Washington.

The captain's voice gets my attention. The PA crackles and I strain to hear his words. Captains do this all the time, announcing our location, altitude, and arrival information. I remove my headset and drop it into my lap. Music seeps into the quiet cabin air. I catch the end of the captain's spiel in his southern Texas drawl.

"As we make our way to Seattle today, our route takes us up the coast."

I return to my book.

"If you look down off to the right, you can see the Air Force base airfield . . ." I'm reaching down to put my headset back on when he says, "Vandenberg Air Force Base, that is." Crystal clear, crisp words.

Wait! Did he just say Vandenberg Air Force Base?

I flash back to my time in Ohio. Over the summer, I stopped at my friend Cindy's house. She was outside in her yard, so I pulled up the driveway to say hi. I was on my way home from the drugstore picking up Mom's prescriptions and didn't have much time, so I simply opened my car door, kept the car running, and chatted over the car roof.

"I thought that was you, Cindy. How are you?"

"I heard about your Mom. Is she doing better?" Cindy dropped her garden hose and moved closer to the car.

"Not really, but thanks for asking."

"How long you in town for? I could try to get some of the girls together for a drink."

"Not sure, I am pretty busy with Mom. Can I give you a call? Let's exchange numbers." The heat from the roof scalds my elbows as I look straight past Cindy toward Adam's house; he used to live next door. I knew he didn't live there anymore, but the residue of him still did as my elbows feel the burn in my heart.

Cindy and I said our goodbyes, exchanged phone numbers, and waved for one last time. Right when I was ducking back into the car, Cindy yelled to me, "His mom told me he's back in the States." Popping back up, I peered at her over the car.

"He's in California at an Air Force base. Vandenberg. You should look him up."

I stood numb, caught off guard by her words, processing them as I looked back at her. Why is she telling me this? Did she see me staring at his house? My smile faded from my face, and I slowly got back in the car, backed out of the driveway, and delivered Mom her prescriptions.

Without my knowing, I suspect that a hundred pilots have told me where Adam is. Flashing back to my flights to and from LA on my way home, the name sounds familiar, but today I allowed myself to hear it. He is right below me where the vast ocean meets the land. I heard it, I know it, now what do I do about it? *Sister, now what are you up to?*

My heart beats at a marching pace, a vital force in my chest digesting the news. My stomach tightens like drying glue, my head rests on the cool glass of the airplane window. I look to the passing clouds for answers and contemplate what to do next. Do I call him? Go see him? Why do I need to do this? What am I searching for? Is this about me, him, or Mom? Do I want to prove Mom wrong? What if she is right? All of these are excuses to call him. It's like trying on an old favorite sweater — not because I want to wear it again but to make sure it still fits. Do I want him to still fit?

In my head, I play out how our conversation might go.

Hi, Adam, remember me? I was your girlfriend in high school. We had a baby — no, we had an abortion. Hi, Adam, I have just one quick question. Did you ever love me?

My daydreaming is interrupted. "Excuse me. Are you off for a few days? On your way home, I hope. Are you doing okay?

I look up at the flight attendant, shaken out of my communion of confessions. "Yes. Sorry, I am off for a few days and on my way home. Can I get a drink, please? A Bloody Mary. These red-eye flights mess me up."

Leaning in, she says, "It's on me. This summer flying is grueling. Enjoy your days off."

Smiling, my cheeks warming up, I glance out the window before I turn back to her again and say, "And yes, I am better than okay. On cloud nine, ten, if that's even possible."

&. &. &.

The plane's wheels screech on the runway surface in Seattle. I am one phone call away from opening the wounds of the past and finally putting them to rest. After I exit the plane, I head home with a bomb in my gut, trying to decide if I should make the phone call when I get there. Do I detonate it and open the war field of emotions, or let it go unlit?

I roll my suitcase from the car into the house, abandoning it in the hallway. Walking straight to my liquor cabinet, I pull down the Stoli bottle, circle back to the kitchen for a glass and ice, and fill it to the rim. Pacing the room, swirling the crackling ice in my glass, Stoli and I have a conversation.

"Call him. You need to know if he loved you."

Answering back to Stoli, "Do I really need to know? Will I prove Mom wrong? Or maybe she is right, he never loved me." *Sister, did the altar boy love me?*

Stoli says, "Let Mom win — she is dying." I collapse into the oversized couch; the phone sits next to me. I look at the clock. It's almost 4:00 p.m. Decision time. If I'm going to call, I need to do it before he leaves for the day. I grab the phone and dial 411 for information.

"4-1-1, city and state please," an operator asks.

"California, is Vandenberg a city?" I say with a question in my voice.

"Party's name?"

"Vandenberg Air Force Base, operator or information number please."

"Would you like the number, or would you like me to connect you?"

"Can I have the number please?" Jumping up, stretching the phone cord to reach my desk, I write the number on a piece of scratch paper. Liquid courage dials the numbers precisely, the phone pressed firmly to my ear. It's ringing. I sit at attention on the couch.

A woman's voice answers. "Vandenberg Air Force Base. How may I direct your call?"

Clearing my throat, I say, "Adam Kelly, please."

"My pleasure. I will connect you to his office."

Thump, thump, thump beats my heart.

Wait.

Is it the right Adam Kelly? How many Adam Kellys are there?

Body twitching, toes tapping, I can't take it anymore. I jump up to pour more courage into my glass; the vodka rattles the ice.

Ringing once, ringing twice, ringing three times, and I exhale a deep sigh as my body resets. Have I escaped detonating the bomb? My pointer finger hovers to end this call. One last ring and then I hear his voice.

"Colonel Adam Kelly speaking." I put my drink down, wiping my sweating palms down the front of my jeans.

My voice is a whisper. "Hello."

Again he says, "Hello."

"Hi. This is Jules Kane. Do you remember me from high school?"

Slowly lowering myself back on the couch, I steady myself, preparing to be a faceless name from the past. Petrified, statue-like, I wait in silence. Anything can happen — anything happens all the time. Stoli and I are hanging up in three, two, one.

"Jules, yes, sorry, you caught me off guard. Of course, yes, I remember you. How could I ever forget?"

His gentle voice is familiar. His calming words crack the statue, and I drop my head, listening to his voice, his words, his breath between sentences.

"How are you? It's been a very long time."

"Good. Yes, it's been a long time." Tell him why you're calling. "I have been spending time in Ohio lately. Someone mentioned you were in California. I hope I called at a good time."

"Yes, perfect time. Just taken off guard. It's not every day I pick up the phone and you are on the other end."

"Maybe this was a bad idea, I shouldn't have called."

"No, that's not what I meant."

"I spend a few weeks a month in LA. If you are ever in the area, maybe we could catch up. I can give you my phone number." I blurt out my number before he answers.

"Yes. Thanks for calling, Jules. Your call is the highlight of my day."

"Goodbye, Colonel," I say, giggling.

"It was very nice hearing your voice again. Thank you again for calling. Bye, Jules."

Gently my finger ends the call, but my heart has other ideas: I don't really want it to end at all.

ᥫᦲ ᥫᦲ ᥫᦲ

Nighttime comes, and in my sleep I wrestle with his voice, his words, his breath between his words. Tossing, turning, cradling myself, I sandwich my ears between my satin pillows. His voice whispers in my ear; his hot breath warms my skin. I exhale into the pillow and can smell his sweetness.

Tortured from not knowing — I should have asked him.

I lie there, tangled between sheets and covers, as morning peers through the curtains. As I lift my head off my pillow, I can feel my hair sticking to my face in a nasty mess. Ringing breaks the quiet, the phone dancing around my nightstand. My head throbs from lack of sleep or too much conversation with Stoli. Blinded by strands of mashed hair, I reach aimlessly across the nightstand, trying to stop the noise that badgers my head. I pick up the receiver, reintroducing silence.

"Hello," I say, my voice crackling.

Waiting for a response, I push the hair off my face and take the phone off my ear to look at the caller ID: 625. Facing the headboard, I jump to my knees, straighten my hair, and cover my naked body, pulling the sheet up to my neck. It's Adam. *Oh, Sister what have I done?*

"I want to see you," his voice rushes out. "I thought about you all night. I can't stop thinking about you."

"Adam?"

"I want to come to LA next week. Will you be there?"

"Yes," I say, clearing my throat, wetting my dry lips. "I will be in El Segundo, just outside LAX, Thursday and Friday."

"Friday would be perfect. I'll drive down after work. If that's okay with you?" he says.

"I hope I can wait that long."

"Do you have a place in mind to meet?"

"The Hacienda Hotel and Bar—it's in El Segundo," I answer. "It would be convenient for me. I can walk there from my place. Call me when you are here, and I will meet you there. I know how LA traffic can be."

"Jules, I can't wait to see you."

I lick my lips with cautious hope, does our love still exist? *Sister, we might have some answers to all my questions very soon. Sister, very soon.*

CHAPTER TWENTY-THREE

Hot water rolls over my body, and the steam billows up to the shower ceiling, masking the fear on my face. My confidence deflating, I slide my back down the shower wall. Sitting under the stream of water, my eyes widen as I realize what is about to happen: I am going to see him in an hour. Does he remember my lips touching his? I remember his soft, supple lips passionately touching mine, forceful and with urgency at first. Once there, they move gently as his lips recognize the comforting tenderness of mine. It felt so good, the way he would hover, barely touching, never wanting to move away.

I stand naked in front of my closet contemplating what to wear, sucking my stomach in while pushing up my boobs. It's too late for a few sit-ups or an aerobics class. Just put something on, I say to myself. *Sister, you had it so easy. One outfit.*

Clothes lie sprawled on the floor, the noes piling up. I riffle through my closet, frantically pushing hangers to the left. *Sister, where is my habit?* My cheeks strain — the smile doesn't want to leave my face as I imagine the look on Adam's face if he were to see me dressed as a nun. Like . . . hmm, is that even a possibility? Do they let divorced, nonvirgin sinners into the convent?

I swoop a form-fitting dark blue dress off its hanger, throw it over my head, and wiggle it down my body. Off-white flowers trim the sleeves, a subtle V-neck displays neither too much nor too little, and the hem settles a few inches above the knee. I zip it up as the silky fabric surrounds my waist. Sliding into my beige high-heeled, strapless sandals, I stand to look in the mirror and tousle my long blonde hair until it's air-dried into soft curls. I grab my small brown purse and throw my keys and lipstick inside before slamming the door shut behind me.

My stomach rumbles, fluttering with nerves and hunger. I realize I haven't eaten today. My heels tap on the concrete sidewalk to the back entrance of the hotel. I make my way up the ramp. Tiles decorated with blue and yellow flowers line the walls.

I walk quietly up the ramp, lifting my heels off the ground like a thief robbing a jewelry store. I need to see him first to settle my heart and prepare my soul. Now on my tippy-toes, I peer around the last corner so I can see into the lobby. I bounce back against the wall's edge, colliding with the person coming around the corner. Off balance, my heels slip beneath me, and my sandal rolls down the ramp. Shaken, I stop, lean against the wall, and gather myself.

"Sorry," I say.

"Jules, is that you?"

I slide my hands down across my hips, straightening my dress. When I raise my head, I meet my collision head-on. The face is familiar. We are not strangers. I extend one hand and then the other. He does the same. My fingertips graze along his palm, my hands gently hold his, and my heart shudders as I inhale his sweet familiar presence.

Enjoying the moment, that simple touch one should never take for granted, I am engulfed by an inner peace that sweeps through my body. He grips tighter, passionately pulling me into his chest while his other hand moves to cradle my head. I rest my head against his beating heart and feel mine in tune with his. We breathe as one, in and out, and I exhale one big sigh of relief. I am back in the ocean, bobbing in the waves, my feet not touching the ground. The tide has washed the calm comfort of him back into my body, just like the first day my eyes met his.

"I hope your name is Adam. You are Adam, right?" I say, laughing out loud.

He squeezes me tighter. "No, who's Adam?"

Leaning back, I look into his eyes, a giant smile on my face. There is no mistake—it's him.

"You are beautiful. Adam is very lucky," he says.

"Drink?" I ask. "The bar is just down this hallway." Turning before he can answer, I walk toward the bar entrance. I try to slow my gait, counting my steps, pace myself . . . one, two, three. My heels tap the terra-cotta tile floor; my dress flows forward and back like willows on a tree.

I scan the Mexican restaurant for a table. The bright red felt-patterned wallpaper dizzies me. My eyes focus on the floor right in front of me as I head for an isolated table across the room. The smell of freshly fried tortilla chips saturates the air. I bounce down into the bench seat. Shimmying my way over to center myself in front of the table, I adjust my dress, cinching it up to cool myself. I watch him walking across the room. He pulls the chair across the tile floor and sits down.

"I need a drink." Then I blurt out. "My mom is dying." Leaning side to side, I try to loosen my dress from the red plastic leather seating beneath me. "She has brain cancer. She's the reason I called you."

He says nothing and looks at me.

I don't know how long the waitress has been standing there, but I suddenly grow aware of her presence. She is staring down at me and Adam. In slow motion, she places two water glasses on the table and waits for the next sentence to come from my mouth or his. He doesn't respond and I don't elaborate. More sweat forms between my thighs. I grab the ice water glass and rub it between my hands, getting more aroused looking at him. *Sister, would he notice if I put the water glass between my legs?*

"Can I get you something else to drink besides water? Dinner, or would you like to start with appetizers?"

"Let's start with drinks. Cabernet for me."

Glancing across the table, Adam responds, "Two, please."

Twirling my ice in its glass, I am drowning. *Sister, this was a bad idea. Why didn't you stop me?* I try to remember why I am here, ignoring the desire tingling through my body.

"I returned to Ohio this year. I had not been home since I was nineteen years old. Did you know that?" Not waiting for a response, I continue with my rambling. "I don't think I would have ever returned home. Ohio, I mean. My mom dying forced me back, forced me to face the past and my feelings about you."

The eavesdropping waitress reappears. Her hand crosses my face and places two glasses of red wine in the middle of the table. My hand quivering, I reach for my glass. Closing my eyes, blindly finding the rim, I take a big gulp.

"Your name was never spoken again in our house. You left, your name left. You left a mess when you went away. I was a mess, and I needed you. I was alone."

"I'm sorry." He peers into his wineglass.

"I had no one to talk to," I continue. "I was repeatedly told that you didn't love me, didn't want me, never wanted me. I started believing it myself, even though I thought we had something different, a tender passion, a connection that was beyond words."

He slowly lifts his head and meets my gaze. "I know I loved you. I always felt like something was missing from my existence, and I've been searching for it.

When I ran into you in the hallway today, I felt it — it came rushing back to me. It was real, very real for me."

Tears roll down my cheeks. "I am here to put the past and the truth behind me, to start healing after so many years of hurt," I begin. "More importantly, to forgive myself for having an abortion and not standing up for myself and for our baby. What we had was magical, something inexplicable and easy. You made me happy. I want to be happy again, and knowing there will never be another you, I need to figure out how to do it alone." I pause and take a deep breath in, long exhale out. "Why did you leave me, Adam? I didn't want to leave you."

The corners of his mouth turn down. He fidgets in his seat and rests his forehead against his fingertips. He shakes his head side to side. His mouth opens, and I lean in to hear. I grab my wineglass, fill my mouth with liquid courage.

He says, "I had no choice. My parents forbade me from seeing you ever again. They told me that is what your parents wanted and that you did not want to see me."

Wine still swirling in my mouth, my brain is drowning in confusion. I stare into the wide-open Mexican bar, not seeing, not feeling, numb. My thoughts flash back to my room, to the counselors, the things Mom would say to me.

"My mother watched me cry myself to sleep, cry for you, and she did nothing. She told me you did not want me, never loved me, used me." Looking past him, I see the door, the exit. I want to run. Run away . . . runway. My life is a lie. My mouth watering, saliva building in my throat, I swallow big. My chin drops. I try to hold back tears.

"Why would she do that?" Adam says. "Jules, I don't have the answers, but we were young and I'm sure our parents just wanted the best for us."

My brain swirls in an ocean of tides; I am trying to tread water and stay afloat. But the current is too strong; it's taking me under. Adam gets up and slides next to me, he wraps his arms around my trembling body, holding me tight, pulling me closer into his cradle.

"I want to kiss away the pain," he whispers in my ear. Gently his fingertips lift my chin. He turns my head and lovingly puts his lips on mine. Melting in this moment, I recall the softness, and my heart slows its beating, relaxed again. The cloud lifts. I was right—it is special.

"I was afraid I would stop breathing before I could kiss these lips again," he says. "I missed your kiss. I was not done loving you. It was not over for me. I missed you every day, missed you everywhere I went, and secretly searched for you all along."

"Adam." Tears of joy roll down my cheeks. Pointing up to the heavens, I whisper inwardly, *Sister, I told you so.*

"I am sorry. I should have fought for you, stayed for you, been there for you. I am here now." Never moving back to his chair, he stays right next to me.

We order another glass of wine. Time escapes us as we try to regain lost time. We carry on crying, laughing, sharing, and always touching, afraid to ever let go.

CHAPTER TWENTY-FOUR

I hear ringing, vibrating — my pager is exploding. I slide my fingers across the warm silk-covered pillowcase in search of my pager above my head. Smiling, I pinch myself to make sure last night was not a dream about Adam. We ended the night by saying good night until next time, never to say good-bye again.

It's Marcella, I reach for the phone to call her.

"Hello." My raspy morning voice crosses through the telephone line.

"Jules, wake up, thanks for calling right away. You need to get home, *now*. Mom has taken a turn; I think it's time. You need to catch a flight today!"

"I think it's time." I have heard those words before. At the hospice, it's code for Mom is going to leave us, it's time to go to heaven and be free from this disease. The hospice nurses seem to know when heaven is peering down closer to those on earth.

I take the first available flight straight to Cleveland. I have five hours to think about Mom, life, death, and now Adam. Words I need to say to her. Words I need to say to free myself from this doubt, this guilt, and to start to fill my heart with joy again. I have come from behind in the race I've been running for way too long. Time to finally cross the finish line. I hope I'm not too late.

Running off the airplane, I head to the baggage claim. I have a car service waiting for me at the curb. Recognizing the car insignia on the side, I run to it. The driver stands at the open trunk. I open the backseat door on my own and slide in, tossing my luggage next to me. He shuts the trunk and slips into the driver seat.

"Nice to see you again, Jules. Where to this time?"

"Same, hospice. Euclid — the one on Lakeside. Please hurry." On-ramps, freeways, familiar side streets all pass in the darkness. The car pulls into the hospice parking lot. As the car rolls to a stop, my door is already open. I toss my suitcase on the ground; the driver's too late to help. I yell back to him, "Bill me. You have my credit card information."

Sister, I have something to say. Please let her hear my words. Let me finish this race. Please let us cross the finish line together with forgiveness.

The bright spotlights illuminating the front door entrance blind me. Squinting to see the clock on the wall, I see the bright red digital numbers glow back at me: 11:07 p.m. The security guard stands at the sound of my ruckus. Greetings usually follow, but this time, he simply straightens his clipboard on the desk. I don't know if he recognizes me or recognizes the look on my face. Panic, fear, death . . . I am sure he has seen it again and again and again. There is no verbal greeting tonight — only a nod in my general direction and a brief meeting of the eyes. I breeze right past him, running with unbounded energy, towing the suitcase behind me. I pass the nurses' station and start to count the doors to Mom's room. One, two, three, four, swinging a wide right into her room, I push forcefully through the door.

My sisters are asleep in chairs spread throughout the room. I try to get a read on the room. Is she still alive? Have I made it in time? They open their tired red eyes, startled by my quick entrance.

Mom is still here, lying in her bed, blankets tucked up high around her neck. Dropping everything, I swiftly move next to her. My own body collapses in relief; my knees drop to the sterile tile floor inching closer to her. Faintly moving my head next to hers, I lightly place it on her shoulder like a baby. Tears roll down my cheeks, relieved that I have made it. *Sister, if you had anything to do with it, thank you.*

I listen to her slow, hollow breath, her bony skeleton body barely accepting each inhale. "Mom, I am here," I whisper. Tenderly, I place my hand on top of her fragile one. Softly I say again, "Mom, it's Jules. I'm here, I made it. I came as soon as I could."

She shifts her fingers below mine. Sluggish and slow movement shows she knows I'm here. She can hear me. Her dry, cracked lips slightly pull apart, her lips barely separate and then close. No sound, only effort. I imagine her voice saying my name. "Jules."

"I can hear you, Mom," I say, holding both of her hands between mine now, nestling in a little closer. "I love you," I whisper softly in her ear. "I am sorry for my failures. I disappointed you." I pause, contemplating my next words. Do I say more?

"Mom, I saw Adam. I know what you did to try to protect me. I did not need protecting. I needed your love, your support, a mom. I was hurt deep inside, and for many reasons, I blamed you. I want you to know I forgive you, but more importantly, the person I needed to forgive is myself, and now I have. I'm going to be okay."

Silence. "Mom, can you still hear me? I saw Adam." Shifting my weight back to my feet, I stand, moving onto the bed next to her. I shiver. A frigid chill has crawled into the room. I tuck her blanket around her shoulders to keep her warm. "Mom, it wasn't over. For either of us and we — "

She squeezes my hand harder this time, her lips separate and move. "Jules, I love you too." This time I can hear her heavenly voice.

She said my name, I heard it.

Her mouth drops wide open. She inhales deeply, followed by rapid gasps for air, her chest barely rising, struggling to bring air into her lungs. I inhale too, a big breath, holding it in, making an extra effort for Mom. We inhale together, one big breath, and her hand slowly loosens around mine. The race is over.

EPILOGUE

Adam and I stayed in contact for twenty-five more years. We tried to make up for lost time, but life's responsibilities got in the way. I learned that sometimes love just isn't enough. It was enough for me, but it takes two to jump off the edge together to make it work. We just never found the right time to jump together. We do love each other in a very special way that can only be explained by how we feel when we are together: selfless joy and calmness. The feeling when you sink your feet into the sand on a summer day and stare out at the synchronized waves rolling in, steady and calm. I still think about him every day, and I believe he thinks about me, but we had to move on and create a life of positive memories with other people.

This book is based on my true story. Names have been changed for privacy, and timelines were altered so my story would flow. I wrote it based on what I can best recall or on what my mind would let me remember. For years I had suppressed memories and intentionally kept them out of my consciousness because they were painful, shameful, and stressful. Writing this book, I opened my mind and my heart, and at times found myself in a very dark place reliving some painful memories. I was able to crawl out. I found forgiveness and reconciled with my mom, whom I loved the whole time. I'm in continual search of happiness and solitude.

I am now a mom, and I understand why my mom did what she did for me. Moms will go to the end of the earth for their children. My mom pushed me to the edge, wanted me to be successful and see the world. I did that, teetering at times, but became stronger and learned along the way. Everyone has a secret, a personal struggle, a heartbreak. If my heart had not been broken, I would never have known what true love feels like. I am blessed. I felt it, and it is the most wonderful feeling in the world. *Sister, it was a journey. The sinner will see you in heaven.*

ABOUT GLIOBLASTOMA

My mother had glioblastoma, a relentless brain cancer. During the writing of this book, an experimental treatment for this cancer was developed, twenty years too late for Mom. My heart goes out to the families and patients with this terrible disease. My mom was taken from me too soon, and I miss her deeply.

31415251R00136

Made in the USA
San Bernardino, CA
04 April 2019